Dear Reader,

Welcome to book two of my duet OUTBACK MARRIAGES. I hope when you've read both stories you'll be able to say with satisfaction, "I really enjoyed them!" Better yet "And I actually learned something I didn't know before!"

A devoted fan recently asked me what inspired me to write so much about the Outback when I wasn't born there. True, I was born in subtropical Brisbane, a city I love, but when I was a girl I went to a prestigious school called All Hallows. All Hallows took in boarders from all over Queensland's vast Outback. These girls had something special about them. When I used to listen to their stories of "home," I was fascinated. They came from places with legendary names like Longreach, Thargominda and Cloncurry, birthplace of QANTAS—Queensland and Northern Territory Aerial Services—and the Royal Flying Doctor Service, which spread its mantle of safety all over the Outback.

I was introduced to billowing red dust storms, drought, flood, the Dreamtime, Aborigines, billabongs, brumbies, camels, dingoes, private planes and governesses when they were small. For the highly imaginative girl I was, the Outback assumed near-mythical proportions in my mind. As a woman I discovered for myself reality not only matched those stories, it exceeded them. I had to see those amazing dry but vivid, burned ocher colors for myself. Our Australian Outback truly does have an incredible mystique. For the majority of you who can't possibly visit, I hope I've succeeded in opening a window on this unique part of the world.

Best wishes to you all, and a very special thank-you to my longtime loyal fans who have given me so much support throughout my long career. If we didn't have readers, we wouldn't have writers! Take a bow!

Margaret Way

She was walking toward him, graciously extending a long, delicate hand.

"How do you do?" she said in a husky voice.

She didn't smile at him, coolly summing him up. He didn't smile at her. Instead they studied one another with an absolute thoroughness that seemed to lock out everyone else in the room.

She looked away first.

He didn't know how to interpret that. A win or a loss?

MARGARET WAY
Cattle Rancher, Convenient Wife

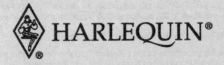

HARLEQUIN®

TORONTO • NEW YORK • LONDON
AMSTERDAM • PARIS • SYDNEY • HAMBURG
STOCKHOLM • ATHENS • TOKYO • MILAN • MADRID
PRAGUE • WARSAW • BUDAPEST • AUCKLAND

ISBN-13: 978-0-373-18283-1
ISBN-10:   0-373-18283-X

CATTLE RANCHER, CONVENIENT WIFE

First North American Publication 2007.

Copyright © 2007 by Margaret Way, Pty., Ltd.

OUTBACK MARRIAGES
These bush bachelors are looking for a bride!

Welcome to Jimboorie—a friendly Outback town that sits amongst the striking red rocky landscape in the heart of Australia. This is where two rugged ranchers begin their quest for marriage.

Meet Clay Cunningham and Rory Compton— they're each searching for a wife. But will they find the right woman with whom to spend the rest of their lives?

Find out in this new duet from Margaret Way!

Last time, you met Clay in
Outback Man Seeks Wife

And now you can read Rory's story!
Cattle Rancher, Convenient Wife

Margaret Way takes great pleasure in her work, and works hard at her pleasure. She enjoys tearing off to the beach with her family on weekends, loves haunting galleries and auctions and is completely given over to French champagne "for every possible joyous occasion." She was born and educated in the river city of Brisbane, Australia, and now lives within sight and sound of beautiful Moreton Bay.

Books by Margaret Way

HARLEQUIN ROMANCE
OUTBACK MAN SEEKS WIFE*
HER OUTBACK PROTECTOR
THE CATTLE BARON'S BRIDE

Outback Marriages

CHAPTER ONE

THOUGH his mood was fairly grim Rory Compton couldn't help but smile. It was the middle of the day, yet a man could fire a cannon down the main street of Jimboorie and not find a target; not even a stray dog. The broad sunlit street was deserted as were the sidewalks, usually ganged on a Saturday. No kids were bobbing, weaving, ducking about, playing some private game, while their mothers, looking harried shouted at them to stop. No one was loading groceries into the family pickup. No dusty four-wheel drive's ran back and forth, the drivers waving casually and calling greetings to friends and acquaintances which meant pretty well everyone in town.

Seated on the upper verandah of Vince Dougherty's pub, Rory had the perfect view of the town centre, its impressive Community Hall and its attractive park. He drained off the cold beer he'd enjoyed with the prepacked lunch Dougherty's wife, Katie, had very kindly left him; a plate of thick roast beef and pickles sandwiches, cling wrapped so well it took him almost five minutes to get into it. He hadn't a hope of working his way through the pile. The stray dog would have come in handy in that regard. With the possible exception of himself, the whole town had taken itself off to the big 'open day' on Jimboorie, an outlying historic sheep station that had given the town its name. Sitting there, his long legs resting on a planter's chair, he debated whether to go. There was a slim chance it could boost his mood.

It was a restoration party he understood from Vince, who being a publican was always ready for a chat that naturally included dramatic revelations. The old homestead, from all accounts, once magnificent, had been allowed to go to rack and ruin under the custodianship of the former owner, Angus Cunningham. 'A miserable old bastard! Didn't think anyone in town was good enough to talk to!'

Of course Rory knew the name Cunningham. The Cunninghams figured among the roll call Outback pioneers. Sheep men. Not cattlemen like his own kind, their stamping ground, the legendary Channel Country, a riverine desert deep into the South-West pocket of their vast State. The new owner, a great nephew, 'one helluva guy!' had spent well over a year and a mountain of money restoring the place. Lucky old him! Vince had invited Rory along to the open day—'Sure and they won't mind!' Vince was as expansive as though he and Cunningham were best mates.

'Maybe,' he'd said. And maybe not. He wasn't in his best spirits since he and his father had had their cataclysmic row a couple of weeks back. Since then he'd been on the road, travelling from one Outback town to another in a sick, angry daze, checking out if there were any pastoral properties on the market he could afford with the help of a hefty bank loan. He couldn't lift his eyes to the multimillion range. All up including the private nest egg his grandad, Trevis Compton, had left him he had close to two million dollars A lot of money to a lot of people. Not near enough when one was talking a halfway decent pastoral property.

'I haven't left your brother, Jay, anything outside the personal things he loves,' Trevis had told him years back. They were sitting on the front steps watching another glorious desert sunset, his grandad's arm around his shoulder. 'Jay's the heir. He gets Turrawin. It's always been that way. The eldest Compton son inherits to ensure the family heritage is kept intact. There are problems with splitting it a number of ways. Jay's a good boy. I love him dearly. But he's not *you*. You're meant for big things, Rory. A little nest egg might well come in handy after I'm gone.'

Rory could still hear his grandfather's deep gentle voice. How could two men be so different? His grandfather and his dad? To be strictly fair his grandfather had led a charmed life with a devoted wife as his constant companion. His son Bernard, however, had his life blighted fairly early. Bitterness ate into a man's soul. That last row had been one row too many. On both sides. His father had sent him on his way—hell he was going anyway— hurling the most vicious and unjust insults that even Rory, used to his father's ungovernable tirades, was deeply shocked. He had passed his elder brother, Jay, his father's heir in the entrance hall.

'Damn him, damn him! Damn him to hell!' Jay was muttering, white faced and shamed, furious with his father for attacking Rory but unprepared to go to his defence. Their father had turned big strong Jay into a powder puff, Rory thought sadly. Anyway Jay's intervention would have been in vain. He was going or his own pride and integrity would be hope-lessly compromised. What did it matter he ran Turrawin these days and largely for the past four years? His father wanted him *out*! Sometimes Rory thought his father couldn't abide to look at him.

They had never been close. Instinctively Rory had known the reason. He strongly resembled his mother who had run off and left her husband and children when Rory was twelve and Jay fourteen.

A *really* bad time. It had brought scandal on the family and a very hard life on Laura Compton's two boys who had worshipped her. From that day forward their father had succumbed to the dark places that were in him. His temper, always volatile became so uncontrollable his young sons lived in a constant state of fear and anxiety. Jay was often in floods of tears after a beating with a riding crop; Rory, *never* which only served to inflame their father further. Both boys regarded boarding school as a god-send. By the age of sixteen and eighteen, both six foot plus, taller and stronger than their father, the beatings had stopped. Their father had been forced to turn his attention back to his whiplash tongue.

'As soon as Dad's dead you and I are going to be full partners,' Jay had promised, his voice full of brotherly love and *pride*. Jay made no bones about it. Rory was everything he was not. 'I won't be able to run Turrawin without you. We both know that. The men look to you not me. *You're* the cattleman. The man to save the station. Dad didn't inherit Grandad's skills or his leadership qualities. Neither did I. You're the *real* cattleman, Rory.'

Rory sighed deeply knowing Jay would get into trouble without him. Bernard Compton had bruised his sons badly. But he hasn't beaten *me*, Rory thought determinedly. I've got everything going for me. Youth, health, strength, the necessary skills. He'd start up his own run. Move up in easy stages. He was as ready to found a dynasty as his Compton ancestors had before him. In time—it would have to be pretty soon, he'd turned twenty-eight—he'd find himself a wife. A young woman reared to the Outback. A woman with a deep love of the land who could withstand an isolated existence without caving in to depression or a mad craving for city lights.

Romantic love wasn't all that high on his agenda. Romance had a shelf life. That was the down side. He had to learn from experience. Most people didn't. History wasn't going to repeat itself with him. His best bet was a *partner* who could go the distance. That meant for *life*; a contractual sort of arrangement that the two of them would honour, working strongly together to build a future. As long as the woman was young and reasonably attractive the sex should be okay. He definitely wanted children. He knew he wasn't and never could be a hard, cruel bastard like his old man. He would be a good father to his children, not bring them up in a minefield. The Outback certainly bred hard men, *tough* men. But mercifully not many like his dad.

So what to do now? Rory stood up and stretched his long arms, staring down at the empty street. He had plenty of time on his hands. Why not take a run out to Jimboorie?

He might as well. Vince had given him directions. A beautiful old homestead would be worth seeing at least. It might even offer some comfort. He'd been intrigued to learn the new owner's Christian name was Clay. Clay Cunningham. He'd only ever met one Clay in his life, but that was a Clay Dyson, the overseer on Havilah a couple of years back. A guy around his own age held in great esteem by his employer, old Colonel Forbes, ex-British Army, now deceased, who had inherited Havilah from his Australian cousin and to everyone's astonishment had remained in the country to work it. Colonel Forbes, universally respected, had thought the world of Clay Dyson, Rory recalled. But it wasn't *that* Clay. Couldn't be. The Clay Dyson he had known had no background of money, no family *name*, though the word was old Colonel Forbes had remembered him in his will.

By the time he arrived on Jimboorie, a splendid property and as far out of his reach as planet Pluto, the main compound was still crowded with people but some were starting to leave making for the parking area crammed with vehicles of all makes and price tags. During the long approach to the station he had seen more than one light aircraft airborne, heading home. He made a quick tour of the very extensive gardens marvelling at the great design and the rich variety of trees, flowering plants and shrubs he presumed were drought tolerant and could withstand dust storms.

Beneath a long tunnel of cerise bouganvillea that blossomed heavily over an all but smothered green wrought-iron trellis, he passed two pretty young women from the town who smiled at him shyly in acknowledgement. He smiled back, raising a hand in salute, totally unaware it only took an instant for his smile to light up his entire face and dispel the dark, serious, brooding look he'd worn since his teens.

Jimboorie House impressed him immensely. He'd never expected it to be so *big* or so grand. It was huge! It rivalled if not surpassed any of the historic homesteads he had been invited into over the years. When his mother had been with them—when they were *family*—they had been invited everywhere as a matter or course. His beautiful mother, Laura, had been very popular, herself an excellent hostess presiding over their own handsome homestead on which she had lavished much love and care.

Why then had she abandoned them? Didn't God decree mothers had to remain with their children? For years he and Jay had accepted the reason their father had drummed into them. City bred their mother had only awaited the opportunity when they were old enough to renounce her lonely Outback life. As young men they came to understand what life for their mother might have been like, though their father had been reasonable enough *then*. Well, for most of the time anyway. He had never actually laid a hand on them when their mother was around except for the odd time when she had protested so strongly he had stopped. In any event she had remarried after the divorce. That happened all the time but it was lousy for the kids.

Their father, as was to be expected given his name, his money and influence, gained custody. He had never been prepared to share it with his ex-wife. The failure of their marriage was her fault entirely. It was one of his father's most marked characteristics, he held himself blameless in all things. Their mother alone deserved condemnation. The sharing was a bad idea anyway. Sensitive Jay had always become enormously upset when it was time to leave her. Equally upset, though he never let on, Rory behaved badly. He had to take the pain out on someone. He had chosen to take it out on his mother. After a while the visits became farther and farther in-between, then ceased altogether.

'Didn't I tell you?' their father had crowed, that hard triumphant gleam in his eyes as he started all over again to trash their mother. 'She doesn't want you. She never did! She's a selfish, self-centred heartless bitch! We're well rid of her!'

Neither of them would have won a good parenting award, Rory thought. But well rid of her? People really did die from grief. All three of them, father and sons, hadn't been able to handle her desertion. Their father, a proud and arrogant man, had never been free of his own grief and crazed thoughts of personal humiliation. Rory's memories of his mother were so heartwrenching he rarely allowed them to touch him. He and Jay had believed their mother to be the sweetest, gentlest, funniest, mother in the world. She could always make them laugh. It just didn't seem possible she had been faking it as their father always claimed. Nevertheless she had left, taking no account of the devastation she left behind her.

In choosing a woman of his own, Rory had long since decided he had to make absolutely sure he kept his eyes and ears open and his feet firmly on the ground. He was as susceptible to a woman's beauty as the next man—maybe more so he thought wryly—but there was no way he was going to allow himself to be seduced by it.

Or so he thought.

Vince Dougherty caught sight of him as he was wandering the grandly proportioned rooms of the old homestead letting it work its magic on him. Whoever had been responsible for the interior decoration— probably a top city designer—had done a great job.

'You made it!' Vince, looking delighted—his enthusiasm was hard to resist—made a beeline for him pumping his hand as though he hadn't seen him for weeks instead of around eight-thirty that morning. 'What d'yah think now? Tell me.' He poked Rory's shoulder which was marginally better than a poke in the ribs. 'You look like a guy with good taste.'

'That's very kind of you, Vince.' Rory's answer was laconic. 'It's magnificent!' His admiration was unfeigned. 'Definitely well worth the visit!'

Vince looked as proud as if he were the owner, decorator, landscaper, all rolled into one. The kind of guy who changed lives. 'Told yah, didn't I? You should have come an hour or so earlier. Meet the Cunninghams yet?'

'Not so far.' Rory shook his head. 'I only came to see the house really. I'm only passing through, Vince. Just like I told you.'

'Well, yah never know!' Vince's face creased into another smile. He was hoping this fine-looking young fella would stay in the district. He glanced upwards to the gallery. 'That's Carrie, Mrs Cunningham up there.' Discreetly he pointed out a blond young woman with a lovely innocent face and a radiant smile. She was standing in the midst of a circle of women friends who were laughing at something she was saying, which they obviously found very funny.

Rory could understand Vince's look of undying admiration. 'She's very beautiful,' he said. 'The house suits her perfectly.'

Vince's big amiable face settled into an expression of pride. 'An angel!' he announced. 'Clay reckons he's the luckiest man in the world. Now how about me taking you to find him? I reckon you young blokes would get on.'

Why not? 'Just point me in his direction, Vince,' Rory said. 'I see your wife beckoning to you.'

'My little sweetheart!' Vince exclaimed, a tag Rory had heard at least forty times during his stay. Vince and Katie were apparently right for each other. Katie wasn't *little*, either. 'Have to get back to the pub sooner or later. Try outdoors, near the fountain. Clay was there a few minutes ago. I don't think he's come back into the house.'

'Will do.' Rory tipped a finger to his temple.

It would turn out to be one of the best moves he had ever made.

The marble three-tiered fountain, monumental in size to suit the grand proportions of the house, was playing; an object of fascination for the children who had to be dragged away from the water by their mothers before they fell in or climbed in as one daring six-year-old had already done and been lightly chastised for. At such times he always remembered how his father had used to bawl him out as a child. It seemed like he had always made his father mad. Madder and madder as the years wore on. And later after their grandad died, the blind rages that took longer and longer to blow over.

A tall, handsome young man stood like a monarch at the top of the broad sloping lawn that ran down to a sun spangled creek. White lilies were blooming all around the banks, an exquisite foil for the sparkling stream and the green foliage of the reeds and the myriad water plants. Rory walked toward him, his spirits growing lighter. Surely it was Clay Dyson? Dyson was an arresting looking guy, hard to miss. Rory let his amazement show on his face.

'It *is* Clay, isn't it? Clay Dyson?' he called. 'Used to be overseer on Havilah a couple of years back?'

The other man turned, his face breaking into a smile of surprise as he recognised his visitor. He walked toward Rory, thrusting out a welcoming hand. 'Cunningham now, Rory. Cunningham is my *real* name by the way. How are you and what are you doing so far from home?' he exclaimed. 'Not that it isn't great to see you.'

'Great to see you!' Rory responded in kind, returning the handshake. He hadn't known Clay Dyson—Cunningham whatever—all that well, but what he'd seen and what he'd heard he'd liked. 'So what's the story, Clay? And this homestead!' He turned to gaze towards the front facade. 'It's magnificent.'

'It is,' Clay agreed with serene pride. 'There is a story, of course. A long one. I'll tell you sometime, but to cut it short it all came about through a bitter family feud. You know about them?'

'I do.' Rory made a wry face.

'Mercifully the feud has been put to bed,' Clay said with satisfaction. 'My great-uncle Angus left me all this.' He threw out his arm with a flourish. 'Caroline, my wife, and I have only recently called a halt to renovations. They were mighty extensive and mighty expensive. What I inherited was a far cry from what you see now.'

'So I believe,' Rory said in an admiring voice. 'I'm staying at the Jimboorie pub for a few days. Vince told me about the open day out here. I'm glad I came.'

'So am I.' Clay smiled. 'Have you met Caroline yet?'

'The very beautiful blonde with the big brown eyes?' Rory gave the other man a sideways grin.

'That's Caroline!' Clay couldn't keep the proud smile off his face.

'I haven't had the pleasure,' Rory said. 'You're one lucky guy, Cunningham.'

'You should talk!' Clay scoffed, totally unaware of Rory's changed circumstances. 'How's Jay isn't it, and your dad?'

'Jay's fine. He's the heir. My dad and I had one helluva bust up. That's why I'm on the road.'

Clay was aware of the pain and anger behind the easy conversational tone. 'That's rough! I'm sorry to hear it.' The Comptons had been an eminent Channel Country cattle family for generations. Where did that leave Rory?

'It was a long time coming,' Rory told him calmly. 'I didn't have any choice but to hit the road. I have some money set aside from my grandad. I guess he knew in his bones I might be in need of it sometime. What I'm looking for now is a spread of my own. Nothing like Jimboorie of course. I'm nowhere in your league, but a nice little run I can bring up to scratch and sell off as I move up the chain.'

Clay looked down to the creek, where children were running and shrieking, overexcited. 'No chance your dad will cool off, Rory? Could there be a reconciliation?'

Rory uncovered his head, his thick wavy hair as black and glossy as a magpie's wing. A lock fell forward on his darkly tanned forehead. 'No way! I wouldn't care if he did. That part of my life is over. The only thing I'm sorry about is I'm leaving Jay to it.'

Clay studied Rory with a thoughtful frown. He remembered now the Compton family history. 'You know I might be able to help you,' Clay confided, like someone who already had an idea in his mind, which indeed he did. 'Why don't you come back inside? Meet Caroline. Stay to dinner. A few friends are stopping over. I'd like you to meet them. You're not desperate to get back to town are you?'

'Heck no!' Rory felt a whole lot better in two minutes flat. 'I'd love to stay if it's okay with your beautiful wife?'

'It'll be fine!' Clay assured him, following his gut feeling about Rory Compton. This was a guy he could trust; a guy who could make a good friend. 'Caroline will be happy to meet you. And we'll have time to catch up.'

'Great!' A surge of pleasure at Clay's hospitality ran through him. Rory whipped out his transforming smile.

Destiny has an amazing way of throwing people together.

CHAPTER TWO

Rory found it all too easy to settle into the spacious, high-ceilinged guest bedroom that had been allotted him. His room at the pub, albeit clean and comfortable was *tiny* for a guy his size.

'Stay the night, Rory,' Clay had insisted. 'We'll be having a few drinks over dinner. Anyway it's too far to drive back into town. Everyone else is staying over until morning. There's any amount of room. Twelve bedrooms in, although we haven't got around to furnishing the lot as yet.'

His bedroom had a beautiful dark hardwood floor, partially covered by a stylish modern rug in cream and brown. Teak furnishings with clean Asian lines gave the room its 'masculine' feel. The colour scheme was elegant and subdued, the bedspread, the drapery fabric and the cushions on the long sofa of a golden beige Thai silk. It was all very classy. Clay had even lent him a shirt to wear to dinner. Something 'dressier' since he'd only been wearing a short-sleeved bush shirt. They were much of a height and build. In fact the shirt fitted perfectly.

Drinks were being served in the refurbished drawing room at seven. It was almost that now. He'd showered and washed his hair using the shampoo in the well-stocked cabinet. Now he gave himself a quick glance in the mirror aware as always of his resemblance to his mother. He had her thick sable hair, her olive skin, though life in the open air had tanned his to bronze. It was *her* eyes looking back at him; the setting, the colour. They flashed silver against his darkened skin. He had her clean bone structure, the high cheekbones, the jawline, stronger and more definite in him. Hell his face was *angular* now he came to take a good look. He'd lost a bit of weight stressing over the current situation and being forever on the road. Who would have ever thought it bad luck to closely resemble his beautiful mother? Although their old man had scarcely liked Jay more, when Jay was almost a double for their father at the same age. Jay could never be brutal. Jay was a lovely human being who really wasn't born to raise cattle. Both straight A students at their 'old money' boarding school Jay had once spoken of a desire to study medicine. It had only brought forth ridicule and high scorn from their father while their mother had gone to Jay laying her smooth cheek against his.

'And you'd be a fine doctor, Jay. Your grandfather Eugene was a highly respected orthopaedic surgeon.'

'Stop it, Laura!' their father had thundered, his handsome face as hard as granite. 'Mollycoddling the boy as usual. Putting ideas into his head. There's no place for nonsense here. Jay is my *heir*! His life is here on Turrawin. Let that be an end to it.'

His expression darkened with remembrance. He missed his brother. Their father would blame Jay for every last little thing that went wrong now. It was dreadful to wish your own father would just ride off into the sunset and never come back, but both of his sons were guilty of wanting that in their minds.

'You *are* a sick bastard, aren't you?' he berated himself, making a huge effort to throw off his mood. He'd already met most of his dinner companions, which was good. No surprises there. They were all nice, friendly people around his age, maybe a year or two older. Two married couples, the Stapletons and the Mastermans and a young woman, called Chloe Sanders with softly curling brown hair and big sky-blue eyes whose face became highly flushed when he spoke to her. Perhaps she was overcome with shyness, though she had to be well into her twenties and maybe past the time for hectic blushes.

It appeared there was a sister, Allegra, who was staying over as well, but so far she hadn't appeared.

Caroline had told him in a quiet aside Allegra, recently divorced, was understandably feeling a bit low. She was staying a while with her mother and sister on the family property, Naroom, which *just could* be up for sale. A hint there surely? The girls' father, Llew Sanders had contracted a very bad strain of malaria while on a visit to New Guinea. Complications had set in but by the time he was properly hospitalised it was already too late. That was six months back, around the time Allegra's divorce had been finalised. All three women had been shattered, Caroline told him, her lovely face compassionate. The daughter who had stayed at home with her parents was Chloe. The one with the fancy name, Allegra, had flown the coup to marry a high flying Sydney stockbroker then had turned around and divorced him within a few years. Rory didn't get it. She was too young for a midlife crisis. Why did she marry at all if she hadn't been prepared to make a go of it? Then again to be fair it might have been the husband's fault? If the sisters looked anything alike, and they probably did, the high flyer husband could well have found someone more glamorous and exciting?

Heaven help me, I might like a bit of glamour and excitement myself!

Rory didn't want to know it, but he was a man at war with himself.

They were all assembled in the drawing room, chatting easily together, drinks in hand.

'Ah, there you are, Rory. What's it to be?' Clay asked. 'I've made a pitcher of ice-cold martinis if you're interested?'

'They're very good!' Meryl Stapleton held up her glass. 'Clay told me his secret. Just show the vermouth bottle to the gin.'

Rory laughed. 'I'm not a great one for cocktails, I'm afraid.'

'A beer then?' Clay produced a top brand.

'Fine.' Rory smiled and went to sit beside Chloe who was sending out silent but unmistakable signals. A man could learn a lot from a woman who wanted him to sit beside her. She flushed up prettily and shifted her rounded bottom to make a place for him. Still no sign of the sister. Perhaps she was all damped down with depression? Maybe their hostess would have to go to her and offer a little encouragement?

Greg Stapleton, a slightly avid expression on his face, immediately started into asking him if he was any relation to the Channel Country Comptons. 'You know the cattle dynasty?'

Obviously Clay hadn't filled him in. Rory was grateful for that. He really didn't want to talk about his family. Nevertheless he found himself nodding casually. 'The very same, Greg.'

'Say that's great!' Greg Stapleton gazed back at

him with heightened interest. 'But what are you doing in this neck of the woods? You'd be way out of your territory?'

Rory answered pleasantly though he wanted to call, 'That's *it*!'

'Actually, Greg, I'm looking to start up on my own.'

Stapleton look amazed. 'Glory be! When Turrawin is one of our major cattle stations? The biggest and the best in the nation. Surely you'd have more than enough to do there?'

'I have an elder brother, Greg,' Rory said, making it sound like it was no big deal instead of a boot out the door situation. 'Jay's my father's heir. Not me. I've always wanted to do my own thing.'

'And I'm sure you'll be marvellous at it,' Chloe spoke up protectively and gently touched his arm. Chloe it appeared was a very sympathetic young woman. Nothing wrong with that!

'I'm totally against this primogeniture thing!' Greg announced. 'It's all wrong and it's hopelessly archaic.'

'Ah, here's Allegra!' Caroline rose gracefully to her feet, grateful for the intervention her guest's arrival presented. Clay had told her in advance a little of Rory Compton's story so she knew he wouldn't want to talk about it. But there was no stopping Greg once he got started. She welcomed the newcomer to their midst. 'Just in time for a drink before dinner, Allegra!'

'That would be lovely!' A faintly husky, marvellously sexy, voice responded.

My God, what a turn up!

Rory just managed to hold himself back from outright staring. He was absolutely certain *this* femme fatale had left not just a husband but a string of broken hearts in her wake. He had enough presence of mind to rise to his feet along with the other men as Chloe's sister walked into the room to join them. No, not walked. It was more like a red carpet glide. How exactly did unexceptional Chloe feel about having this beautiful exotic creature for a sister? All Rory's sympathies were with Chloe. The sisters couldn't have looked less alike. He hoped Chloe wasn't jealous. Jealousy was a hell of a thing to haul around.

In a split second his dazzlement turned to an intense wariness and even a lick of sexual antagonism that appeared out of nowhere. It wasn't admirable and it stunned him. He wasn't usually *this* judgemental.

She was a redhead. Not Titian. A much deeper shade. More the lustrous red one saw in the heart of a garnet, a stone he recalled had been sacred to ancient civilisations such as the Aztecs and the Mayans. She wore her hair long and flowing. He liked that. Most men would. It curved away from her face and fell over her shoulders like a shining cape.

It even lifted most glamorously in the evening breeze that wafted through the French doors. Her eyes were a jewelled topaz-blue, set in a thick fringe of dark lashes. Her skin wasn't the pale porcelain usually seen in redheads. It had an alluring tint of gold. Very very *smooth*. Probably she dyed her hair. That would explain the skin tones. Her hair was an extraordinary colour.

She was much taller than Chloe with a body as slender and pliant as a lily. Her yellow silk dress was perfectly simple, yet to him it oozed style. He might have been staring at some beautiful young woman who modelled high couture clothes for a living or something equally frivolous like spinning the wheel on a quiz show.

'You know everyone except Rory,' Caroline was saying, happy to make the introduction. 'Allegra this is Rory Compton who hails from the Channel Country. Rory, this is Chloe's sister, Allegra Hamilton.'

She was walking towards him, graciously extending a long delicate hand. What was he supposed to do, fall to one knee? Kiss the air above her fingers? Powerful attraction often went along with a rush of contrary emotions, or so he had read. 'How do you do,' she said in that husky voice, as though equally struck by something in him she didn't quite understand, or for that matter *like*.

It might have been a gale force wind instead of a breeze blowing through the open doors. Rory swallowed hard on the roaring in his ears. What the hell! One could shake hands with a vision. Get it over. Life went on. He knew he hadn't imagined the shiver of electricity. It was a wonder they hadn't struck sparks off one another. It happened. But there was bound to be a scientific explanation. He felt more comfortable with that, though he hadn't the slightest doubt she could cause such a response at will.

Well ma'am, I survived it!

She didn't smile at him, coolly summing him up. He didn't smile at her. Instead they studied one another with an absolute thoroughness that seemed to lock out everyone else in the room.

She looked away first.

He didn't know how to interpret that. A win or a loss?

Over dinner, it turned out stunning Allegra was also smart. Pretty soon he'd be lost in admiration. Light-hearted conversation set the tone for most of the meal. They talked about anything and everything. A recent art auction, remarkable for the high prices paid for aboriginal art, music, classical and pop, favourite films, books, celebrities in the news, steering clear of anything confrontational. He liked the way she entered spiritedly into the discussions, revealing not only a broad general knowledge, but a wicked sense of humour. Now why should that surprise him? Rory had to chide himself for being so damned chauvinistic in the face of the twenty-first century. Why shouldn't there be a good brain behind that beautiful exterior? His mother had been a clever woman, well educated, well read. Not much of a mother, however, as it turned out. Not all glorious looking women kept themselves busy luring rich guys into marriage he reminded himself.

What *really* struck him, was the way sweet little Chloe kept heckling her sister just about every time she opened her mouth. Heckling was the only way he could interpret it. It was all done with a cutesy smile, which he thought rather odd, but towards the end he found himself fed up with it. Sisterly ease and friendliness appeared to be a thin veneer.

On the other hand—further surprising him— there appeared to be no limit to Allegra's tolerance. She had such a high mettled look to her and surely a redhead's temper he had expected a free-for-all. If again that gorgeous mane was natural? But never once did she retaliate to her sister's running inter-ference when Rory had thought of a few sharp answers himself. There was no way Chloe could be totally free of jealousy, he reasoned. Poor Chloe. This was one of the ways she handled it.

'And what's your feeling, Rory?' Allegra startled

him by addressing him directly. She looked across the gleaming table, her beauty quite electrifying amid the candlelight and flowers.

'I'm sorry, I missed that.' *I was too damned busy wondering about you!*

She smiled as though aware of it. 'We were talking about the mystery resignation.' She named a well-known politician who had stunned everyone including the prime minister by vacating his federal seat literally overnight.

'He's had a breakdown, I'd say,' Rory offered quietly, after a moment of reflection.

'Doesn't look like that to me.' Greg Stapleton's mouth curled into a sardonic grin. 'Could be woman trouble. The man looks great, fit and well. I saw him only recently on a talk show. He's a good-looking bloke, happily married supposedly. One of the top performers in government.'

'A high achiever,' Rory agreed. 'And he *is* happily married, with three children. He is a man who drives himself hard. When depression hits it hits hard. It can hit anyone. I've met the man and really admired him.'

'So you think all the stress that goes along with the job—the lengthy periods away from home— got to him?' Allegra asked, studying Rory very carefully and obviously waiting on his answer.

'That's my opinion,' he said. 'But I'm prepared to bet he is the man to confront it and win out.'

She gave a gratifying nod of approval. 'I'm sure we all wish him well.'

Chloe at this point, not to be outdone, attempted to start a rousing political discussion, which was met not so much with disinterest but a disinclination to spoil the mood. Subdued she turned her attention back to cutting down her sister at the same time keeping her own brain underwraps. Appearances could be very deceptive Rory was fast learning. He'd initially thought sweet Chloe would make some man a good wife. Perhaps she *would*. Just so long as her sister wasn't around.

Irritations aside, dinner went off very well. A roulade of salmon with a crab cream sauce; smoked duck breast as a change from beef, a lime and ginger brulée. Someone took an excellent approach to cooking. He hadn't been eating well on the road. Clay and his beautiful wife were the best of hosts; the formal dining room recently redecorated and refurbished was splendid and the food and wine matched up.

It was well after midnight before they broke up. Rory was one of the last to make his way upstairs to his guest room because he and Clay had a private conversation first.

'If you want I could have a word with Allegra in the morning,' Clay suggested, drawing Rory into the book filled library. 'There's a possibility the Sanders property—it's called Naroom by the way—could come on the market.'

'You think they're serious?' Rory asked, staggered by all the leatherbound tomes. Did anyone read them?

'We won't exactly know until I broach the subject.'

'Why Allegra, why not both sisters?' Rory asked, fairly cautiously.

Clay's response was dry. 'Not to be unkind, you've met both sisters. Allegra is definitely the brains of the outfit.'

'Is that why Chloe's so darned resentful?' Rory's chiselled mouth twisted.

'I've never seen Chloe quite so bad,' Clay confessed. '*You* might have had something to do with that!' A teasing grin split his face.

'Cut it out!' Rory's voice was wry. 'I'm sure Chloe can be a very nice person when she tries, but I have to say I'm not interested.'

'What about Allegra?' Clay continued, tongue-in-cheek. 'She's so much more beautiful—'

'And brainier,' Rory cut in. 'Sorry, I know what a beautiful woman can do to a man. You're one of the lucky ones.'

'About as lucky as a man can get,' Clay admitted with a smile. 'Anyway, who could blame Chloe for being so miffed. Allegra has so much going for her.'

'Really?' Rory raised a brow. 'I thought she'd just come out of an unpleasant divorce?'

'So she has. I think she's been feeling a bit down lately. Who could blame her?'

'That must account for the way she hasn't got around to telling her little sister to back off?'

'It's all about sibling rivalry, my man!' Clay groaned. 'Anyway if you like I'll suss out the situation for you in the morning. No harm done one way or the other, but I'm pretty sure they'll want to sell. I'll see what Allegra has to say and let you know.'

'That'll be great, Clay. I much appreciate what you're doing for me and thank you again for your splendid hospitality.'

'A pleasure!' Clay's smile was wide and genuine.

Afterwards Rory found himself following the lingerers, Allegra and Chloe up the grand staircase quite unable to prevent himself from admiring Allegra's long slender legs and delicate ankles. Never in his wildest dreams had he anticipated meeting a woman like this. To try to do something about it would be madness. He was a man looking for a suitable woman to make his wife. He'd be a total fool to lift his eyes to a goddess who found mortal men dull in a very short time.

He was so engrossed in his thoughts, half admiration, half remonstration, when he almost barged into her. As surefooted as a gazelle, she suddenly stumbled, throwing out a slender ringless hand he had already observed over dinner, to clutch at the banister.

'Oh heavens!' she gasped, sounding relieved he had broken her fall.

'Okay?' Rory's arm shot out like lightning. With his arm around her, his whole body went electric with tension. He dared not even open his mouth again. Instead he stared into her disturbingly beautiful face, unaware his eyes had gone as brilliant and hard as any diamonds.

'She's sloshed!' Chloe explained, looking at her sister aghast.

Rory found himself jumping to Allegra's defence. 'Nothing like it!' His answer came out a shade too curtly, causing poor Chloe to colour up. Allegra Hamilton had had no more than three glasses of wine over the space of the whole evening. He knew that for a fact. He'd rarely taken his eyes off her, which could only mean he had more need of caution.

As it was, he held her lightly but very carefully, surprised the silk dress she wore wasn't going up in smoke. He was searingly aware of the pliant curves and contours of her body. He could smell her perfume. A man could ruin himself over a woman like this. He fully understood that. He just bet she haunted the ex-husband's dreams, poor devil!

'Do you feel faint?' he asked, studying her pale oval face.

Chloe looked on speechlessly.

For a moment Allegra's dazzling gaze locked on his, then when she couldn't hold his gaze any longer, she shook her head as if in an effort to clear it. 'Just a little. It will pass.'

'She doesn't eat,' Chloe informed him like it was an ill kept secret. Her face and neck were flushed with colour. 'Anorexia, you know. Or near enough. So she can wear all those tight clothes.'

Now that just *could* be right, Rory thought. She had eaten lightly at dinner. She was as willowy as a reed. He should know. He still had his arm around her. It felt incredibly, dangerously *intimate*. Anyone would think he'd never had his arm around a woman in his life. He was no monk. But he was, he realised to his extreme discomfort, consumed by the warmth of this woman's body and the lovely fragrance it gave off. It blurred his objective faculties, casting a subversive spell. Allegra Hamilton was a heartbreaker. He knew all about *those*.

'Lord, Chloe, will you stop making it up as you go along. I'm *not* anorexic,' Allegra sighed. 'Though I confess I haven't had much appetite of late. Or much sleep. Thank you, Rory. I'm fine now.' It was said with the faintest trace of acid as though she was aware of the erotic thoughts that were running through his head. She shook back her hair, squared her shoulders and slowly straightened up. 'It was just a fuzzy moment. Nothing to get alarmed about.'

'How many times have I heard you say that after a dinner party?' Chloe directed a tight conspiratorial smile in Rory's direction.

'The fact is you've *never* heard it, Chloe,' Allegra answered with a kind of weary resignation.

'I have, too,' Chloe suddenly barked. 'Mark was really worried about your drinking.'

Allegra laughed shakily. 'What, Diet Coke?'

'Why don't I just carry you to your room?' Rory suggested, not at all happy with the way she was near dragging herself up the stairs, one hand on the banister. He didn't want to hear about her ex-husband, either. Not tonight anyway. 'You'd be as light as a feather.'

'You're kidding!' She paused to give him a vaguely taunting glance. 'A feather?'

'If I pick you up I can prove it. You look to me like you need carrying to your room.' Before she could say another word or get out a word of protest, he scooped her up in his arms.

'There, what did I tell you?' His voice mocked her, but in reality he was seized by a feeling of intoxication that was enormously distracting. It came at him in mounting waves. For one forbidden moment he went hot with desire, quite without the power to cool it. Never before had a woman stirred such a response. His every other experience paled into insignificance beside this. A man of good sense should fear such things as not all that long ago men feared witches.

She caught her breath, astounded by his action. Then she gave way to laughter. 'A woman has to be careful around you I can see, Rory Compton. I've never been swept off my feet before. Though it does fit your image.'

'What image?' He looked down at her with his brooding, light filled eyes.

'Man of action. It's written all over you.'

'Look I'm really sorry, Rory,' Chloe said, trotting in their wake. 'Allegra is always doing things like this. It's so embarrassing.'

'Give me a break, Chloe!' Allegra broke into a moan before she was overcome again by laughter. Peals of it. It simply took her over. 'I've never met a man like Rhett Butler before,' she gasped.

Though her mood seemed lighthearted, Rory had the odd feeling she was on the verge of tears. A woman's tears could render a man very vulnerable. He knew when she was alone in her room they might flow.

With his arms around her body, her beautiful face so close, excitement was pouring into him way beyond the level of comfort. Wariness had turned to wonder. Wonder to a dark, albeit *involuntary* desire. She might have been naked in his arms so acutely did his senses respond.

Oh ye of little resolve! A taunting voice started up in his head. But then he hadn't seen a woman like Allegra Hamilton coming.

What he needed now was a long, cold bracing shower. She was an incredibly desirable woman yet he was half appalled by his own reactions, the depth and dimension, the sheer physical pleasure he took in holding her. The breasts he couldn't help but look down on, were small but beautifully shaped; her shoulders delicately feminine. Her arched neck had the elegance of a swan's. What would a man feel like carrying a woman such as this to their bridal bed? It came to him with a fierce jolt he deeply resented the fact another man had already done so. How could that same man bring himself to let her go? He didn't really know but he was prepared to bet it was she who had tossed her husband aside. And how many other men had she ensnared before him?

It was more than time to set her down before she totally messed him up.

Chloe ran ahead helpfully and opened the bedroom door. 'Anyone would think she was a baby. She can walk.' She looked up at Rory sympathetically. 'Just put her on the bed.'

My God, didn't he want to!

He was no damned different from all the other poor fools. Whatever his mind said, whatever his will demanded, underneath he was just a man whose fate was to succumb to woman.

'Please, Chloe,' Allegra laughed. 'I'm the wronged party. It's this cowboy who swept me off my feet.'

'Cattleman, ma'am,' he corrected, now so perversely hostile he barely stopped himself from pitching her onto the huge four-poster bed, its timber glowing honey-gold.

'Rory, I didn't mean to offend you,' she apologised, still caught between laughter and tears.

'Forgive me, I think you did.' He couldn't say he badly resented being put under a spell. He wasn't accustomed to such things.

'I confess I find *your* attitude a little worrying, too.' From a lying position—God how erotic—she sat up on the bed, staring at him with her great topaz-blue eyes.

'Hey, what on earth are you two talking about?' Chloe was struggling hard to keep up. It all seemed incomprehensible to her.

'Nothing. Absolutely nothing,' Rory said, further perplexing her. Allegra Hamilton in the space of one evening had got right under his skin. He was aware his muscles had gone rigid with the effort not to yield to the urge to lean forward, close the space between them, grasp those delicate shoulders and kiss her hard. Only desiring a woman like that was an option he simply couldn't afford.

Maybe it was her utter unattainability that made her so desirable to him? He had to find a reason to give him comfort. On his way to the door Rory turned to give her one last glance.

A big mistake!

She couldn't have looked more ravishing or the setting more marvellously appropriate. The quilted bedspread gleamed an opulent gold, embroidered with richly coloured flowers. Her dress had ridden up over her lovely legs, pooling around her in deep yellow. Her hair shone a rich red beneath an antique gilt and crystal chandelier that hung from a central rose in the plastered ceiling. Hanging over the head of the bed was a very beautiful flower painting of yellow roses in a brass bowl, lit from above.

It was enough to steal any man's breath away.

'Good night, Rory,' she said sweetly, which he translated into, 'Goodbye!'

He nodded his dark head curtly, but made no response.

Witch!

She was accustomed to putting men under a spell. But for all he knew she could have a heart of ice.

Coming as he did from the desert where there was a much higher pitch of light and the vast landscape was so brilliantly coloured, Rory found his trip out to Naroom, enjoyable, but relatively uninspiring compared to his own region, the Channel Country. The bones of many dead men lay beneath the fiery iron-oxide red soil of his nearly eight hundred thousand square kilometre desert domain. The explorers Burke and Wills had perished there; the great Charles Sturt, the first explorer to ever enter the Simpson Desert almost came to final grief—the German Ludwig Leichhardt became a victim of the forbidding landscape. Not only had the early explorers been challenged by that wild land, but so too were the pioneering cattlemen like his forebears who had followed. After good rains, the best cattle fattening country in the world, in times of drought they had to exploit the water in the Great Artesian Basin, which lay beneath the Simpson Desert to keep their vast herds alive. And exploitation was the word. It really worried him that one day the flow of water to the several natural springs and the artificial bores might cease. What a calamity!

To Rory, the desert atmosphere of home was so vivid he could smell it and taste it on his tongue. These vast central plains seemed much nearer civilisation. He had lived all his life in a riverine desert, bordered on Turrawin's west by the one hundred thousand square kilometre Simpson Desert of central Australia. His world was a world of infinite horizons and maybe because of it, the desert possessed an extraordinary mystique.

It was certainly a different world from the silvery plains he was driving through. His landscapes were surreal. They seeped into a man's soul. The desert was where he belonged, he thought sadly, though he accepted it was fearsome country compared to those gentler, more tranquil landscapes; the silvers, the browns, the dark sapphires and the sage-greens. He was used to a sun scorched land where the shifting red sands were decorated with bright golden clumps of Spinifex that glowed at dusk. Scenically the Channel Country was not duplicated by any other region on the continent. It was unique.

Unique, too, the way the desert, universally a bold fiery-red, was literally smothered in wildflowers of all colours after the rains. No matter what ailed him such sights had always offered him relief, a safety valve after grim exchanges with his father, even a considerable degree of healing. There were just some places one *belonged*. Fate had made him a second son and given him a father who had shown himself to be without heart. He was the second son who was neither wanted nor needed.

Well let it lie.

Clay as promised had set up this meeting with the Sanders women. Clay would have come along, only he was fathoms deep in work. Rory would have liked his company—they got on extremely well together—but he didn't mind. It was just the two sisters and their mother. An exploratory chat. Just the two sisters? Who was he kidding? He couldn't wait to lay eyes on Allegra Hamilton again. In fact it hadn't been easy putting her out of his mind.

You can handle it, he told himself.

With no conviction whatever.

Clay had assured him Mrs Sanders *was* seriously considering selling, although the property wasn't on the market as yet. Clay, during his conversation with the beauteous Mrs Hamilton, had formed the idea the family would want between $3.5 and $4 million, although she hadn't given much away. Clay got the impression Allegra didn't really want to sell.

Why not? It wasn't as though a woman like that, a hothouse orchid, could work the place. Nevertheless Rory had already taken the opportunity of having a long, private phone conversation with one of Turrawin's bankers. A man he was used to and who knew him and his capabilities. He had been given the go-ahead on a sizeable loan to match his own equity. Naroom wasn't a big property as properties in his part of the world went—nowhere near the size of Jimboorie for that matter, let alone Turrawin. The property from all accounts had been allowed to run down following the death of Llew Sanders and the unexpected departure of their overseer who it was rumoured had had a falling out with Mrs Sanders. A woman who 'kept herself to herself' and consequently wasn't much liked. Rory wanted to ask where Allegra had got her extraordinary looks from, but thought it unfair to Chloe who seemed a nice little thing if she could just hurdle the sibling rivalry or trade in her present life for a new one.

Rivalry simply hadn't existed between him and Jay. They had always been the best of friends. The strong bond formed in early childhood had only grown closer with the changing circumstances of their lives. In many ways he had taken on the mantle of older brother even though he was two years Jay's junior. He had shielded the quieter, more sensitive Jay through their traumatic adolescence and gone on to take the burden away from Jay in the running of the station. That old hypocrite, his father, had been well aware of it but chose—because it suited him— to keep his mouth and his purse shut.

Valerie Sanders walked into the kitchen in time to see Allegra taking a tray of chocolate chip cookies out of the oven, presumably to offer to their visitor with tea or coffee. Cooking wasn't Valerie's forte so she had left Allegra to it. Besides she had sacked their housekeeper, Beth, who didn't know how to keep a still tongue in her head, even after fourteen years.

'I hope you're not going to be difficult, Allegra,' Valerie, a trim and attractive fifty-two-year-old now said, picking up their discussion from breakfast. 'I want the place sold. So does Chloe. Why should you care? You don't live here. You have to stop thinking of yourself for a change.'

Allegra transferred the cookies to a wire cooling rack before answering. She had learned long ago to ignore Valerie's perennial sniping. Crossing swords with her only reinforced it. 'That's a bit unfair, Val,' she said mildly. 'All I said was, we can't simply *give* Naroom away. It's worth every penny of $4 million even if it's not the best of times to sell. Dad would turn over in his grave if we sold it for less. It just seemed to me you and Chloe are prepared to accept the first offer.'

Valerie's light blue gaze turned baleful. 'I want *out*, Allegra. I've had more than enough of life on the land and Chloe has had *no* life at all. I know you don't worry about your sister. But she has to find a good man to marry and she isn't getting any younger. You had a good man and you were fool enough to let him get away.'

Allegra refused to fire. 'Do you actually listen to a word I say, Val? Mark was unfaithful to me. Since when are philanderers good men?' She busied herself setting out cups and saucers. 'As for Chloe, I used to invite her to stay with us often enough. Surely you remember?'

'How could she stay when there was always

tension between you and Mark?' Valerie retaliated. 'Though it must be said Mark always did his best to pretend nothing was wrong. Chloe and I have come to the conclusion *you* were the source of all the trouble, Allegra, however much you protest. And you've always gone out of your way to put your sister in the shade. You could have been a real help to her, but you live in your own little world.'

Allegra couldn't help a groan escaping her. 'So you've been pointing out to me for years and years. Now we're on the subject of Chloe, she's not much help around the place. I hear her complaining about putting on weight when the surefire answer is exercise. There's plenty to do around the house since you let Beth go.'

'We couldn't afford her,' Valerie said briefly.

'She been with us for years and years,' Allegra said, thankful she had managed to contact Beth who was now living with her sister

'That awful woman!' Beth, her anger up, had raged. 'I only stayed because of your dad. It was all so different when you left home, Ally love. Personally I think your stepmother drove your poor dear father bonkers! He must have spent years of his life wondering why he married her.'

He married her for my sake, Allegra thought sadly. To give me a mother.

'Now when this young man arrives I want you to

stay in the background,' Valerie said. 'If such a thing is possible. Your father spoilt you terribly.'

'I suppose he was trying to make up for you, Val,' Allegra offered dryly. 'I've always irritated the living daylights out of you.' In fact Allegra couldn't recall a happy, carefree period of her life; a time when she was not exposed to Valerie's shrouded antagonism, which nevertheless Allegra was made aware of even as a child.

'So you have,' Valerie admitted. 'You must have irritated the living daylights out of Mark as well. You could have held onto him with a little understanding. We all know men are in the habit of having a bit on the side But your ego couldn't tolerate that, could it?'

Allegra considered this, aghast. 'My ego had nothing to do with it. Dad didn't have a bit on the side as you phrase it.'

'No, he was faithful to the memory of your sainted mother!' At long last Valerie gave vent to the helpless anger she'd been forced to stifle for years; anger that had at its heart jealousy of a ghost.

'Now you've come out with it.' Allegra experienced a hard pang. 'I can see from now on it's going to be no-holds-barred. That's the answer to all our woes, isn't it? I'm guilty of resembling my mother who died before she was thirty. Think about that, Val. You're *jealous* of a woman who died so young? Would you have swapped places with her? It's truly sad, but you've never been able to master your deep envy of her place in Dad's life. The fact I look so much like her has only made you fixate on it all these long years. I suppose it was inevitable.'

'Psychoanalyst now are we?' Valerie jeered, her expression bitter. 'Actually I'm fine. Llew is dead. Naroom will soon be sold. It was never really *my* home. More *her* shrine. No need for us to put up a pretence anymore. But don't kid yourself. The conflicts we've had over the years have been caused by your pushing me or your sister to the limit. I wasn't your darling mummy. You were such an assertive child, always demanding your father's attention. You took your demands to the next stage with your husband. Small wonder he left you.'

'Oh go jump, Val!' Allegra had come to the end of her tether. '*I* left Mark. But don't let's upset your mind-set.'

'Mark told me *you* made him feel alienated,' Valerie persisted.

'Since when did you become Mark's champion?' Allegra asked wearily. 'He's ancient history, Val.'

The expression on Valerie's face was one of primitive antagonism. 'Alienation was the cause of much of his unhappiness and his turning to someone else.'

Allegra groaned with frustration. 'You're talking through your hat. It was more than some*one* else, Val.'

'I bet you had your little flings as well,' Valerie

quickly countered. 'You demand constant admiration.'

'None of which has ever been handed out by you. Some stepmothers are wonderful. Heaps of them! But your crowning achievement has been picking on me. All your love has been given to your own child. I had to lean heavily on Dad. You set out early to drive a wedge between me and Chloe. You bred your own resentment into her. As for my marriage, I respected my vows.'

Valerie gave a mocking smile. 'The reason I understand exactly what Mark meant when he said you alienated him is because you alienate *me*.'

'Then I'm sorry!' Allegra threw up her hands, thinking her stepmother's problems with her would never be resolved until the family—such as it was—split up. Her father had held them all together. Now he was gone. 'I have to get changed,' she said, moving towards the door. 'Rory Compton should be here soon.'

'Set to fascinate him, are we?' Valerie called after her.

The facade of caring stepmother was rapidly crumbling.

In her bedroom Allegra changed out of the loose dress she'd been wearing since breakfast into a cool top with a gypsy style skirt that created a breeze around her legs. She slung a silver studded belt around her narrow waist and hunted up a pair of turquoise sandals to match her outfit. It was second nature to her to try to look her best no matter how she felt. For one thing her job as Fashion Editor on a glossy magazine demanded it. Besides, looking good gave her the extra confidence she needed. It helped her present her best face to the world.

Inside, these days, she felt totally derailed. Her beloved father gone. The only person in the world who had truly loved her. Val coming out into the open, spitting chips! No husband to be there for her. What does a woman do when she can't keep her husband of three years faithful? So much for beauty! She had thought in her naivete, she and Mark would be together for life—Mark the father of her children—but she and Mark had been marching to a very different tune. Fidelity simply wasn't in his nature, though he had given every outward semblance of it for quite a while. That was until she received in the mail a batch of photographs, stunning evidence of her husband's betrayal. They were sent anonymously of course. Not a single word accompanied them as though the photographs said it all; which indeed they did. They were from someone who didn't so much care about her pain as showing Mark up for what he was. Allegra had always had the idea that person was a woman.

Someone who may have been a former lover of Mark's and now hated him.

Mark's explanation when she had confronted him with them had been quite extraordinary. He had acted calm, as though he couldn't quite grasp her devastating shock.

'It's long over, Ally!' He'd assured her in his smooth, convincing stockbroker's voice. 'It meant absolutely nothing. All it did was relieve a physical ache at the time. Let's face it, my darling, I don't get as much sex from you, as I want, though I have to admit it increases your allure. Why do women make such a big deal about men having extra needs? It's *you* I love. You're my *wife*. No other woman can touch you. I'll never leave you and you'll never leave me. I'd be devastated if you did.'

She was the one who was devastated but, God help her, she had forgiven him. It was too early in their marriage to call it a day. She certainly couldn't go home to Val to seek advice and comfort. She told herself lots of people make mistakes. She made herself believe it had been Mark's only infidelity. In retrospect, of course it hadn't been. Mark was addicted to sex like another man might have been addicted to golf. It was a necessary relaxation, a *fix*. Mark was handsome, charming, successful, generous. Especially with his favours.

In the beginning he had been a tender, sensitive,

romantic lover, eager to please her. She realised now what he had been doing was gradually trying to break her in to his little ways she found vaguely demeaning, though she tried to understand where he was coming from. It wasn't as though there was much harm in what he wanted her to do it. It wasn't even overpoweringly sensual. But she couldn't help feeling titillating little games were ridiculous. Certainly they didn't turn her on.

'Sweetheart, you're not a bit of fun!'

Seeing how she felt, he backed off. Overnight he rectified his behaviour, which had never been evident during their courtship, returning to the considerate, caring lover. She'd believed like a fool they had come to an understanding. Nothing further was going to be allowed to disrupt their lives. Only Mark secretly moved back to the kind of women who were up for the kind of sexual kicks he craved. The other women turned out to be married women from their own circle. Why had she been so shocked? Faithless friends made faithless lovers. All of them had been exceedingly careful, not wanting exposure or even to break up their existing marriages. There was no wild partying, no staying out overnight, much less for long weekends. Their marriage might have survived for quite a bit longer only she had returned home from work unexpectedly early one afternoon only to find Mark and a married friend of theirs chasing one another around the bedroom.

Incredibly she hadn't been laid low. She hadn't screamed or cried or yelled at the woman to get dressed and get the hell out of her house. For a moment she had very nearly laughed. They looked so ridiculous staring back at her. Like a pair of startled kangaroos caught in the headlights of a four-wheel drive.

'Goodness, Penny, I scarcely recognised you without your clothes!'

Then she had turned about and walked straight out of the house, booking into a hotel.

So here she was at twenty-seven, a betrayed wife. A betrayed ex-wife. And having a hard time coming to terms with what a fool she had been. She had truly believed Mark was a man of integrity. Yet love or what she thought had been love had flown out the window. Indeed it had all but taken wing when she had first received those compromising photographs with her clever handsome husband caught in the act, his unflattering position preventing her from seeing his partner-in-crime's face. At one stage, as she bent over the photographs, she had the weirdest notion that partner could have been Chloe—something about the slight plumpness of the legs, what she could see of the woman's body?—but quickly rejected the idea, disgusted with herself for even allowing such a notion to cross her mind. Chloe would never do such a thing. Chloe was far too honourable.

Incredibly Mark had tried desperately to save their marriage, saying she was making something out of nothing. Just how did one define *nothing*? A man wasn't intended to remain monogamous, he said. Everyone knew that. Smart women accepted it; turned a blind eye.

He obviously didn't want to consider the innumerable crimes of passion that hit the headlines. He continued to hold to the line he 'adored' her. He knew he had a problem of sorts, but he would seek counselling if that's what she wanted. They would go together.

She had declined without regrets. She had to face the dismal fact Mark was highly unlikely to be cured. Sooner or later he would break out again. He had found it ridiculously easy up to date. Almost ten years her senior and well versed in the less laudable ways of the world, he had run rings around her. Even after their divorce became final he had stalked her, telling her how ashamed he was of his behaviour and how much he desperately needed her. Didn't he deserve another chance?

Tell me. Whatever it is you want me to do, I'll do it. I've already entered into treatment.

She knew it was a lie. The only thing Mark was sorry about was getting *caught*.

Why had she married him in the first place? He hadn't exactly swept her off her feet, though he couldn't have been kinder, sweeter, or more considerate. His intellect had reached out to her. He was a clever, cultured man, highly successful with powerful friends. She went from single woman with no *real* home—home with Valerie and had felt like enemy territory—to married woman with a beautiful home of her own and an extraordinarily generous husband who showered her with gifts. Was that what she had really wanted all along?

A home of her own?

She never told anyone about Mark's little idiosyncrasies. She could well be confiding in someone who already knew. She didn't blacken his name. She knew quite a few in their circle believed she was the one to bring what had appeared to be a marriage made in heaven to an abrupt end. Mark was 'a lovely guy!' Everyone knew he adored her. The age difference might have had something to do with it. Or Allegra had found someone else. In her work she was invited everywhere with or without her husband—there had to be lots of temptations along the way, men and women behaving the way they did.

Allegra knew people had been talking, but there was little she could do about it but take it on the chin.

CHAPTER THREE

RORY COMPTON had already arrived by the time she made her way downstairs. She realized with a prickle of something like discomfort and an irrational guilt she had taken a few extra little pains with her appearance. She was aware too of a quickening of excitement that was gathering in strength. She hadn't expected anything like it. Not here, not *now*. Not when she wanted time to re-evaluate her life. She was a woman trying to recover from a recent divorce. Sad things had happened to her, leaving her feeling low, but the advent of Rory Compton into her life had sparked off some sort of revival. Without wanting to, or without planning it, he had somehow brought her back to life. Could it possibly have something to do with the rebound syndrome? She had actually seen it at work with a friend. Women were very vulnerable after the break-up of a relationship. Was she one of them?

Since she had met him she had started to ask

herself that very question. She couldn't stop thinking of him though she had willed herself not to. But like all things forbidden he had stuck in her mind. There was just something about the man that had penetrated the miasma of grief she had been battling since the death of her beloved father and the failure of her marriage. She had been certain in her mind she wanted to remain untouchable. At least for a proper period of time. In a sense she was mourning the death of her marriage; the death of a dream.

Rory Compton had changed all that and in a remarkably short space of time. She would do well to see the danger in that. All it had needed was a glance from his remarkable eyes; the peculiar excitement she had felt when he had swept her up into his arms; the way her heart rate had speeded up. He had drawn from her not only a physical, but an emotional response. It wasn't simply his arresting looks. She had really liked the way he had been at the Cunningham's dinner party; his sense of humour, his broad range of interests and the sympathy and sensitivity he had shown towards the politician, a fellow man battling the depression that had fallen on him so unexpectedly.

Rory Compton was formidable, she had concluded. A real presence for a man his age. There was something very purposeful and intent about him and she had to concede a hidden anger, or at the very least brooding. He had actually made her feel like her old self. Correction. More like she was running at full throttle. Was it the adversarial look in those silver frosted eyes? Or the taunting half smile? He was physically very strong. He had lifted her as though she weighed no more than a twelve-year-old. She sensed his physical attraction to her—given that it was quite involuntary—maddened him. Here was a man who liked to be in control.

Holding her in his arms had quite spoilt it for him. The truth was—she couldn't hide it from herself— she had been as aroused as he was. Powerful physical attraction was a daunting thing, especially when it came out of left field. She would do well to be wary of it. Once bitten, twice shy? What did she know of him after all? Her judgement had been way off with Mark. She wasn't about to make a habit of it. She needed to know much more about Rory Compton. It would be better given her background to mistrust rather than trust.

What you're feeling, girl, are hormones. You have to let it pass.

He was seated on the verandah at the white wicker table. Valerie and Chloe flanked him, both looking surprisingly mellow. Chloe too had gone to some pains, Allegra thought gently. Her apple blossom skin that flushed easily heightened the colour of her eyes and she was wearing a very pretty dress Allegra had brought with her as a present, knowing exactly what would best suit her sister.

Allegra paused for a moment in the open doorway, hoping she had given them enough time alone with their visitor as requested, though requested was too polite a word.

Immediately Rory Compton saw her he sprang to his feet, the man of dark compelling looks she too vividly remembered. A wedge of crow-black hair had fallen forwards on his forehead giving him a very attractive, slightly rakish look. Worn longer than was usual, his glossy, thick textured hair curled up at his nape. It would be great hair to touch. His eyes glittered against his bronze skin. Today his cheekbones looked more pronounced. There wasn't a skerrick of weight on him. His nose was very straight above his beautifully cut mouth. Not generously full lipped like Mark's, but firm and chiselled. He had the sort of face one wouldn't forget in a hurry.

Despite her little pep talks to herself she forgot about betrayal, failure and the tense situation that existed between her and Valerie. She pretended she was considering a particularly sexy man to act as the foil for the beautiful female model in a fashion shoot. No question he would get the job. Two or three inches over six feet, by and large he was moving from lean to nearly thin even in the couple of days since she had last seen him. It startled her to realise it, but something about him caught at her heart. It was a sentiment that in its tenderness took her completely by surprise. This man was eating away at her defences. No wonder she felt a tingle of alarm.

As on the first occasion when they had been introduced, he didn't smile and he had a wonderful smile. She'd seen it directed at Chloe among others. She didn't smile, either, and there was nothing wrong with *her* smile. Instead she inclined her head in acknowledgement of his presence. Both of them matched up in self-protectiveness, she thought. Perversely she wondered as her eyes alighted on his mouth what it would be like to kiss those chiselled lips?

Don't think about it!

She had nothing to hope for with Rory Compton. He was a near stranger It was the wrong time for starting another relationship anyway, though she couldn't help but be aware there was *something* between them.

'Mrs Hamilton!' He inclined his dark head in greeting.

'Please, Allegra.' It came out more coolly than she intended. She planned to drop the Hamilton anyway.

'Well now we'd almost given up on you!' Val announced, as though Allegra was habitually late and consciously rude.

'Why is that, Val?'

Rory held a chair for her. He hadn't been expecting to hear her call her mother by her Christian name, or to mark the swirling undercurrents now they were together. This wasn't one close-knit family, he swiftly intuited. Chloe had no problem with 'Mum.' In fact Chloe was sweetly affectionate towards her mother and her mother clearly doted on her. That wasn't the case, it seemed, with her elder daughter.

'Well you did tell us you had plenty of other things to do,' Chloe started into a deliberate lie. Why did men have to look at Allegra the way they did? It brought out the worst in her.

'Like making coffee or tea?' Allegra looked down on her sister's silky brown head. 'Would you like to come and help me?' *Since when?* When there was a job to be done it had never taken Chloe long to disappear. Born and reared on a working station Chloe had no love of the outdoor life or work of any kind. As a girl she had always wanted to stay at home with Mum who had never encouraged Chloe to pull her weight.

Valerie, as was her practice, jumped in on Chloe's behalf. 'Chloe has opted to take Rory for a drive around the property. But we would like coffee first. Coffee for you, Rory? Or tea if you prefer?' Valerie smiled at this extraordinarily personable young man. Chloe had already told her how strikingly handsome he was. Not to mention those eyes!

Rory, however, turned to Allegra. She was so damned magnetic he decided there and then caution had to determine his every response. 'Coffee's fine,' he said. 'Sure *I* can't help you bring it out?'

Some imp of mischief got into Allegra. 'Thank you so much,' she said gracefully. 'Please come through.' She turned to lead the way, but not before catching the glare in Valerie's eyes.

Under the terms of her father's will his estate had been split three ways, but not in the way any of them had expected. Certainly not Valerie. She and Chloe had each inherited quarter shares; Allegra half, much to Valerie's outrage.

If I want to invite this man into the house I have a perfect right to do so no matter the scowl on Valerie's face, Allegra thought. Her father's will had further alienated her from her family when she had thought their mutual loss would bring them closer together.

Faint hope! She knew Valerie and Chloe believed she had received a handsome divorce settlement from Mark but she had refused to take a penny. How could she do such a thing? The choice to end the marriage had been hers. She wanted nothing of Mark's, even the beautiful jewellery he had given her. She hadn't even opted to take her wedding ring let alone the magnificent solitaire diamond engagement ring. He could save that for her successor.

* * *

Rory followed her into the large well equipped kitchen, definitely troubled by the undercurrents. He was surprised Allegra—who looked like she was used to being waited on hand and foot—was the one to organise the morning tea. He really had to stop being so quick with his assumptions Blame it on his unnatural bias.

'Coffee, you said?' She gave him a glance that just stopped short of challenge.

He understood because he felt the same powerful urge to challenge her. He didn't understand exactly why, but he did know everything had changed since he had met her. 'Yes, thank you.' He looked about him. 'You have a very attractive home.'

'It actually needs refurbishing,' she said, setting the percolator on the hot plate. 'Nothing has been touched since my mother redecorated it in the early days of her marriage.'

That meant well over twenty years surely? Chloe had told him that first evening she was twenty-three to Allegra's twenty-seven. She had made twenty-seven sound more like seventy-two. 'She hasn't felt the urge to try her hand again?' he asked. 'I thought women loved rearranging things.'

Allegra sliced into the fruit cake she had made the previous day. 'So we do, but my mother, sadly, is no longer with us. She was killed in a car crash when I was a toddler. I would have been killed, too, only it was one of the rare times I wasn't with her.'

Initially he felt shock, then an explanation for the things that were troubling him. 'I'm very sorry for your loss,' he said with sincerity. 'So Valerie is your stepmother?'

'And Chloe my half sister,' she nodded. 'My father remarried when I was three. A lot of people think Val is my mother because she's always been there.'

He looked at her keenly. 'But she wasn't the mother you wanted?'

She took a few moments to answer. 'You're going to psychoanalyse me?'

'No, just a question.'

'Why would you *say* that?' She wasn't surprised, however, by his perception.

He gave a self-deprecating shrug. 'I'm an authority on mothers that go missing. Mine left home when I was twelve and my brother, Jay, fourteen.'

'And the reason, seeing we're cutting right through the usual preliminaries?'

'She couldn't take it anymore,' he offered bluntly.

'She was having marital problems?' Allegra began to load the trolley.

'You would know about them,' he answered in a low dark voice.

'Indeed I do,' she returned smartly.

'Yes, she was having problems,' he admitted,

thinking the very air scintillated around her. 'My father was and remains a very difficult man.'

'You look like you might have a few hang-ups of your own?' She stopped what she was doing and pinned him with her gaze

'Thanks for noticing,' he said suavely.

'Don't feel bad about it. I have them as well. So name one.'

'I don't trust beautiful women.'

Her stomach did a little flip. He could say that yet it was as if he had reached out and kissed her. 'Never in this world?' Somehow she managed a smile.

'No.' Slowly he shook his head, not breaking the eye contact.

'Wow!' The expression on her face was both satirical and amused. 'We're going to have lots to talk about. I don't trust handsome men.'

'I understood your ex-husband adored you?' Now that was definitely a challenge.

'We had different ideas about what being 'adored' meant. I think you actually *did* adore your mother?'

His eyes turned as turbulent as a stormy sea. 'We both did. Jay and I. Seen from our point of view her leaving was an abandonment.'

'But you see her now?' she asked, fully expecting the answer to be yes.

He picked up three lemons and juggled them in

his sure hands. 'Not for many years,' he said and returned the lemons to the bowl. 'Close on fifteen.'

'Good grief!' She didn't hide her surprise. 'So you haven't seen her since you were a boy?' She wondered how that could have been allowed to happen.

He held aloof. 'That's right, Mrs Hamilton.' He focused on watching her move around the kitchen. She was very efficient in her movements. In fact she was perfectly at home in a kitchen when he had been too ready to think she was the quintessential hothouse flower who lay about gracefully while someone else did the work.

'Allegra,' she corrected, speaking sharply because he was unnerving her and he knew it. 'Sorry, I don't care for Mrs Hamilton,' she said more calmly. 'You don't feel motivated to find her?'

He didn't hesitate. 'No. But I know where she is.'

She had to suck air into her lungs. 'You make it sound like the outer reaches of the galaxy.'

'Might as well be.' Rory had to steady himself, too, unwilling for her to see just how much the old trauma still hurt. 'It's a long, hard road back from betrayal, *Allegra*.' He placed mocking emphasis on her name.

She studied his handsome, brooding face for a moment. 'Isn't it strange how we punish the ones we love? You're absolutely sure you know the reason? She must have been desperately unhappy?'

He took so long to answer she thought he was

going to ignore her question. 'That's there under the abandonment,' he conceded. 'I guess she was unhappy. For a *while* at least.' He put a mocking hand to his heart, his luminous eyes dangerously bright. 'She remarried a couple of years later.'

'Life goes on.' She shrugged. 'So did my dad, but he never forgot my mother. One of the reasons he remarried so soon was that he needed a wife to look after me.'

And what a beautiful child she must have been! Rory let his gaze rest on her, aware his fingers were curled tight into his palms as though he might make some involuntary move towards her. A woman like that any man could lose his senses. But to let himself fall in love with her would be one hell of an ill fated idea. She had wonderful skin, wonderful colouring. He allowed his eyes, at least, to barely skim the low neckline of her top. It dipped as she moved, revealing the satin-smooth upper curves of her breasts. The blue of that clingy little top was the same colour as her eyes. Of course she knew that. She wore her mane of garnet hair in a classic knot. And it *was* natural. Abandoning indifference if only for a moment he had asked Chloe. Chloe said the only nice thing she had said about her sister all night. 'Yes, isn't it beautiful! Hair that colour is rare!'

The sheer power of a beautiful woman!. A lover

of beauty in all its forms, Rory felt himself drenched in heat. He had to realise he was achingly vulnerable to this particular woman. A woman like that could take a lot off a man without giving a thing back.

Belatedly he picked up the conversation. 'And that woman was Valerie?'

'Yes.' Allegra for her part, didn't fully understand why this man moved her like he did. It was as though she could see through the layers of defences accumulated through the years, to when he was a handsome, daring little boy. A little boy who had the capacity to be badly hurt.

'A lot of expectations were put on her,' he said.

'Absolutely!' Her answer was faintly bitter in response to the irony of his tone.

'It can't be an easy job trying to raise another woman's child?' He looked at her, lifting a black brow.

'No one suggested it was,' she said bluntly.

'Okay, I'll back off.'

'Do.' She was frosty in her tone. 'To get off the subject, I might as well tell you I've read up on Compton Holdings. I'll ask a few questions of my own now, if I may? Why did you leave? Surely with a huge enterprise and a flagship station like Turrawin there was more than enough room and work for two brothers? Or a dozen brothers for that matter.'

His expression hardened. 'For most people there

would be, but you haven't met my father. My father is a very controlling sort of man and I'm long past marching to his drumbeat. I needed to strike out on my own.'

'Then you have the money to buy here?' She resorted to a brisk business-like tone.

'Always supposing I'm interested.' His eyes mocked her. 'I haven't seen over the place yet.'

'You wouldn't be here if you thought it a waste of time, but I warn you I'm no push-over, Rory Compton.'

'Excuse me, *you* inherited?' He leaned back nonchalantly against a cabinet and folded his arms.

What a combination of male graces he had, such an elegance of movement. 'I'm the major shareholder,' she informed him coolly, aware of something else. He offered torment as well as poignancy.

'That's unusual?'

'Well *you'd* know all about that.' She came back spiritedly.

'Touché!' Unexpectedly he gave her his rare smile. It was so heartbreaking it was just as well it came and went fairly rarely. 'I think we got off on the wrong foot, Allegra.'

She wanted to remain as cool as a cucumber but the way he said her name tugged at her heart. Perversely it reminded her of the need for caution. How could her interest in a man reawaken so quickly after her divorce? The answer? This man was too compelling. 'That happens when people are wary of one another, ' she said.

'*Are* we?' he asked , feigning a wondering voice. Neither of them could deny there was a strong current running between them.

'Isn't that the word you would use?' She kept her eyes on him. No struggle at all.

'As I say, it pays to be wary around a beautiful woman.' Impatiently he slicked that troublesome stray lock back. 'Did I mention I find you beautiful?' Well, she knew that for a fact. No harm in getting it out into the open.

'That worries you?' Her blue eyes checked on his expression.

'Terribly.' He smiled.

The really extraordinary thing was she smiled back. 'Whatever looks I have they haven't done me much good,' she said wryly.

'But I understood from Chloe you're a fashion editor on a magazine? If they wanted someone to look the part you had to be it.'

'Why thank you, Rory.'

He smiled. 'If I know anything about women, it's they like to be complimented now and then.'

'True. Okay, my looks were important there,' she conceded. 'But I wanted a happy marriage far more than a successful career. I wanted children. I wanted family. I wanted years and years and years of watching my kids grow up. I wanted grandchildren. I wanted my husband and myself to grow old together, still in love.'

He gave her a searching look. 'A lot of wants, Allegra. You didn't try for a family?' God a man would so want a child with her.

There was pain in her expression. 'You don't know when to quit do you? That's a very personal question.'

'Maybe, but I'm in pursuit of truth here. It so happens, I'm looking for a wife.'

Her heart did a somersault in her breast. 'Is that your next career move?' Somehow she gave the question an edge of sarcasm.

'Sure is. Total commitment,' he confirmed.

'Don't dare look at *me*.' She issued the warning with a little laugh. 'I won't be thinking of marriage for a long, long time.'

'Afraid?'

'You bet!' she answered swiftly. 'I made one mistake. I'm sure you'll appreciate I'll be very cautious about making another. To be honest, Rory, I didn't see *your* offer coming.' She gave him a sparkling glance.

'I didn't make one, did I? Hell, I'm as cautious as you, Allegra. But I have to tell you, you impress me.' He made a mock study of her as though she were a possible candidate. 'You're a highly desirable woman in any man's language, but there's that wary bit we both share.'

'Maybe you'd be more in tune with Chloe?' she suggested. 'And here I was thinking you were simply looking to buy a property?'

'But I am,' he assured her. 'It was you who introduced the subject telling me you wanted children. I feel the same way I want a wife and family. It's predictable I suppose. I never really had one.'

'So what's wrong with advertising?' she suggested helpfully.

'Nothing whatsoever,' he said. 'We guys live in such isolation it's not easy to find partners.'

'I understand that,' she said, 'having been reared on the land. I have a feeling, though, if you do advertise you'll be inundated with answers.'

'I'm counting on it. In the meantime, there's *you*!' He flickered a silver glance at her.

It was pathetic, but thrills ran down her spine. 'It's like I told you, Rory Compton. Count me out!'

His handsome face was openly mocking. 'I know better than to argue.'

'That's a relief.' She felt a flush over her whole body.

Footsteps echoed in the hallway. In the next minute Chloe bustled in, eyes wide as she tried to gauge the atmosphere. From the look that came over her face she could have suspected amazing sex on the kitchen table. 'What in the world are you doing?' she asked, transferring her glance from one to the other.

'My fault,' Rory said, and flashed Allegra a smile.

Chloe's cheeks smarted. 'I just thought you might need some help?'

'We're fine thanks, Chloe,' Allegra said pleasantly. 'You can play Mother and wheel the trolley out if you like.'

Forty minutes later Rory was sitting in the passenger seat of the station Jeep with Chloe at the wheel. So far he could see work around Naroom had all but come to a stop. Why wouldn't it without an overseer to run it? Whatever had persuaded Mrs Sanders to sack her late husband's right hand man? It didn't make sense unless that was confirmation she had no intention of remaining on the land. Even then it was counter productive to allow the property to decline. He had seen around the homestead and liked it. It was spacious, comfortable, attractive. The outbuildings for the most part were in good condition. Now he asked Chloe to stop while he spoke to one of the stockmen who was driving a small mob of healthy looking beasts towards the creek.

'We'd be mighty pleased if a good man could buy the place,' the stockman confided within minutes of Rory's calling out to him. He was only too ready to talk and hopefully hold on to his job. 'Things have gone from bad to worse since the Boss died and Jack left. Jack Nelson was the overseer here for the past ten years with no complaints from the Boss, but Jack and the Missus couldn't see eye to eye. Or even half an eye come to that. She never wanted to spend any money maintaining the place. It was a real battle trying to get any money out of her for anything, even paying the vet. Jack reckoned she was only waiting for a buyer so she could sell up. The only one who loves the place is Miss Allegra. Miss Chloe now—I can see her back there in the Jeep—you want to strap yourself in—she won't do no rough work. Not much of a rider, either, which is pretty funny when to see Miss Allegra in the saddle does a man's heart good. She can handle most of the jobs on the station, too. Her dad taught her. Chloe, now, always liked to spend her time indoors with her mum. Both of them are bone lazy if you ask me. Hell, don't tell her that. I could lose my job.' He shut up abruptly.

Back in the Jeep Rory would have liked to suggest he take over the driving but didn't want to hurt Chloe's feelings. She didn't so much steer as wrestle with the wheel. One of her little foibles was hitting as many pot holes and partially submerged rocks as she could, sniffing them out like a heat-seeking missile. It was almost as if it were her bounden duty. Then she groaned aloud as the vehicle reacted with a stomach churning kangarooing. Excuses ranged from, 'Whoops, didn't see that!' to 'That wasn't there last time!' Maintenance on the Jeep would run heavily to shock absorbers he reckoned.

'What did Gallagher have to say?' she asked when they resumed their seats after another bout of catapulting.

Rory thought it better not to pass on Gallagher's indiscretions. 'Nothing much. Just saying hello.'

'It's a wonder Mum didn't sack him along with Jack Nelson,' Chloe muttered, incredibly clipping a branch of a tree.

'Why's that?' Rory wondered how Chloe could possibly drive in a city or even a small town without hitting everything in her path. He even began to wonder if she'd had any proper driving lessons or simply got behind the wheel one day without bothering about lessons or a licence. He recalled he and Jay could drive around the station from a very early age.

'Cheeky bugger! Not respectful enough to Mum or me.' Chloe bridled.

'Who, Nelson or Gallagher?' Both that voice in his head said.

'Both,' Chloe confirmed, her pretty mouth tightening. 'It would be wonderful if you really liked the place, Rory. No one ever thought Dad would die so young. Mum and I are lost without him. Running a station needs a man. Dad needed a son. Instead he got Allegra and me,' she said wryly. 'I stayed. I was the loyal one. Allegra cleared off as soon as she could.'

'Oh, yes, when was this?' He tried not to sound too interested when he found himself avid for information.

'She insisted on going to university while I had to stay at home. Mum needed me. It's so lonely out here a girl could go ape. Afterwards Allegra landed a magazine job. We all know why. She's the perfect clothes horse and she *does* have good taste although it took a few years before she got the big promotion.'

'Was this before or after she married?' Rory asked, intrigued Allegra might have kept working when she had married a rich man.

'The promotion?' She took such a lengthy look at him, Rory was forced to put a steadying hand on the wheel.

'Yes.'

Chloe placed her hand gently over his and took a while to take it off. 'She was fashion editor when she met Mark. She could easily have quit her job and devoted herself to being a good wife to Mark, but she didn't. I think a man deserves that, don't you? He's *such* a lovely man, too, and she *dumped* him. I ask you! Dump the love of your life?'

'Obviously he wasn't,' Rory suggested, not trying all that hard to dull the sarcasm.

'Seems not,' Chloe sighed and headed into a clump of brambles. 'Mum and I really took to him. He's so handsome and clever *and* rich and he worshipped her. It's a bit weird isn't it the way men worship beautiful women? I mean beauty's only a tiny fraction of what a real woman is all about. I tell you when she left him Mum and I were gobsmacked. We even thought he might top himself.'

'Surely not!' Rory groaned before he could help himself. 'Your father liked him, too?' He wanted some perspective on the worshipping husband. Not that he exactly blamed him, tiny fraction or not.

Pretty Chloe scowled darkly. 'Oh, as far as Dad was concerned no one was good enough for Allegra!' she said, her voice betraying her intense jealousy. 'You've no idea what it was like for me when we were growing up. Allegra always wanting the attention and getting it from Dad. Allegra could be an absolute *pig*!' She paused a moment to cool down. She didn't want Rory getting the wrong idea about her. 'We're half sisters, you know.'

'Allegra did tell me,.' Rory admitted, surprised they were any relation at all.

'She would. No matter how much Mum and I tried she would never let us love her and Mum's the sweetest woman who ever drew breath.'

Rory fought a wry smile.

'I hesitate to say this,' Chloe continued with some

relish, 'in fact it hurts me, but it might help you understand. My beautiful sister is pretty shallow. I don't think there's a man alive who could make her happy.' To reinforce her opinion Chloe hit the steering wheel with her open palm.

Sibling rivalry could be absolutely deadly Rory thought. Potentially so could Chloe's driving. 'That's your opinion, Chloe, is it? And what about you?' Rory kept his eyes glued ahead for more likely obstacles. If he'd only known what going for a drive with Chloe held in store! 'What are your plans if and when the station is sold?'

Chloe swung her head to beam at him. A woman just waiting to be hit by Cupid's arrow. 'I'm going to find myself a man,' she confessed with a dimpled grin. 'I'm going to have a Big White Wedding I'll always remember. And I won't have Allegra for my damned bridesmaid,' she tacked on wrathfully, heading towards a solitary gum tree like it was a designated pit stop. 'You can be sure of that!'.

Rory gently nudged the wheel. 'Obviously a sore point?' The reason wasn't lost on him.

'Well, I won't want her upstaging me on the best day of my life.' Inexplicably she braked hard as if they were coming to a set of traffic lights mysteriously erected in the bush. 'Can you blame me?' Satisfied about whatever it was—he didn't have a clue—she picked up speed again. 'I won't even let her meet my husband until after we're married just to be on the safe side. I won't be like her, either. Sadly she could only stay married five minutes. Marriage is forever, Rory, don't you think?'

He must have lost a layer of skin. Either that or it was the way Chloe was affecting him. 'Absolutely,' he said, 'or I'd want my money back.'

They insisted he stay for a late lunch again prepared and served by Allegra who, as far as Rory could see, could get a job at a top restaurant.

'Great meal, Allegra,' he complimented her. In fact it was the best meal he'd had for quite a while, outside dinner with the Cunninghams.

Chloe blushed fiercely. 'It's only a chicken dish,' she pointed out with a flick of the head, though she had not only overloaded her plate she had scoffed the lot.

'The secret's in the spices,' Allegra told him, ignoring her sister, instead of giving her the thump on the back of the head she deserved. 'I'd be glad to give you the recipe to hand on.'

'Perfect,' he said.

'Hand on ? Who to?' Chloe looked baffled, staring from one to the other in an effort to get them to divulge the secret.

'Rory is compiling a cookbook to hand over to his future wife,' Allegra said.

'Good heavens! Are you really?' Chloe looked fascinated by such a thing. After all she had a glory box.

'I hadn't been thinking of it,' Rory confessed. 'Now I'm convinced I should do it.'

'Anyone special in your life, Rory?' Valerie asked, irritated beyond measure by the constant exchanges between their visitor and Allegra and trying none too successfully not to show it.

He shook his head. 'No, not really, Mrs. Sanders.' He gave her an easy smile.

'What's wrong with all the girls then?' Valerie favoured him with a girlish one of her own. 'I would have thought you'd be fighting them off?'

Chloe, mouth slightly open, looked like she felt exactly the same way.

'A man doesn't get to meet too many where I come from,' Rory explained. 'The desert is about as remote as one can get.'

'Well then I'm sure you'll do better here,' Valerie said with great satisfaction, aiming a fond glance in her daughter's direction.

Rory vowed there and then not to give Chloe the slightest encouragement.

He took his leave of them thirty minutes later saying he'd have to think things over before getting back to them.

'Naturally' Valerie smiled and touched him

gently on the arm. 'We have to put our heads together, too.'

'Walk out to the car with me.' Rory managed to get off a quick aside to Allegra as Valerie wheeled about to have a word—never mind what it was—with her daughter.

'Very well.' Allegra led the way down the front steps, fully expecting Chloe to seize the moment and race after them. All right, Chloe didn't normally race, but there was always the first time. She had obviously taken a shine to Rory. Even Valerie had broken out into sunny smiles. One had to be a good looking young man to get one.

Strangely Chloe didn't come after them. There was only one explanation. It was too hot. 'So do you want to tell me your thoughts now?' she asked as Rory fell in alongside her. She really liked the way she had to look up to him. In her high heels she and Mark had been fairly level.

'Your stepmother made a huge tactical error sacking your overseer,' he commented in a crisp voice.

'Tell me something I don't know,' she sighed. 'Jack got on with everybody.' Except Valerie.

'Obviously he found it pretty hard going with your stepmother.'

Not wanting to criticise Valerie, Allegra said nothing.

'Surely you have a big stake in seeing the place

is run properly?' Rory prompted, looking down at her flaming head. For some reason—again beyond him—he felt he could talk to her like he'd known her for ever. She was tall for a woman, around five-eight but to him she *felt* small. Indeed he'd had extreme difficulty keeping the *feel* of her out of his dreams. But there was no way he could volunteer that.

'That's why I'm here.' She showed a little flash of temper. 'Losing Dad was a great blow for all of us. Dad was the one who held us all together. With him gone I'm very much afraid I'll be minus what family I have left. Val and I never did get on.'

'Actually I can understand that,' he said laconically.

When Val had been on her best behaviour, Allegra thought. He should come on them unexpectedly. 'The thing is I was fatally blemished in my step-mother's eyes because I resemble my mother. Val suffered from the second wife syndrome. It's a very hurtful and wounding situation.'

Rory nodded. 'Skewed by the dagger of jealousy! Have you all come to some agreement on an asking price?'

'Not as yet,' she said.

'You *are* going to be able to work it out, right?' he asked dryly.

'Don't worry, we will. I take it you feel you can do something with the place?'

'Not feel, *know*,' he said, sounding utterly confident.

'Ah, the arrogance of achievement!' she said. 'Word is *you* ran your family station?'

'Jay and I.' He put her straight. 'I love my brother.'

'But he's not the cattleman in the family?'

'Would you believe he wanted to be a doctor?'

She picked up on the sadness, the regret. 'So, what stopped him? What finer calling could there be?'

'He's my father's heir, Allegra,' he pointed out. 'That says it all.'

'Okay. I understand. And I don't.' For total strangers they had moved quickly to a very real communication, no matter how edgy. 'It seems to me Jay should have fought for his dream, instead of letting it die a slow death.'

'Only life has a way of falling short of our dreams,' he said, ever sensitive to any criticism of his brother. 'So what decided you to scuttle *your* dream?' he questioned, combining a real desire to know with that little flash of sexual hostility.

'Scuttle is entirely the wrong word.' She gave him her own admonishing glance. 'I wanted to *cure* the situation. My dream was to find harmony and fulfilment. I thought I had a fighting chance with Mark but it blew up in my face like Krakatoa.'

'So you took the only course open to you. You bolted?' He was determined to know.

'What does anyone do when they find out they've made a big mistake,' she asked, very soberly. 'Now

I've got to get my life back on track. Incidentally I'm stunned I'm talking like this to a near stranger.'

'It *is* a bit eerie,' he agreed. 'I'm not always like this with strange women, either. Then again we can think of it as pouring out a life story to the person sitting next to us on a plane.'

She laughed. 'I assure you I've never done it. There's too much to you, Rory Compton. Darkness, Lightness. Now I think back, I realise I was running away. I love Naroom. I love station life. After all it's what I was bred to. Yet I was impelled to change my life. It wasn't the best reason to marry.'

'You obviously weren't prepared to stick it out for the next forty years.'

It was said in a voice that so infuriated her, she wanted to slap him. 'It strikes me that's none of your business.'

'True. It's just that I'm dying to know. How long was it again?'

'I repeat. None of your business, Compton,' she returned coolly. 'You don't approve of what I did, do you?' She came to a standstill staring up into his dynamic face.

He almost reached out to tuck a stray lock of her hair behind her ear. 'I don't approve of divorce in general, Allegra, being a child of divorce. Not unless there's a very good and pressing reason. Which you may well have. Forgive me for not minding my own business.'

'You know what they say. Curiosity killed the cat.'

'Curiosity isn't the right word. It implies a passing interest. I aspire to seeing more of you, Miss Allegra. For better or worse, we seem to have bonded. I haven't as yet figured out why. There's one thing jumps to mind. Your cooking. A woman's ability to put out a good meal finds high favour with most men. Other things about you, however, could scare me.'

She acknowledged the mocking glitter in his eyes with a tight smile. 'It's hard to believe any woman could scare you. By the way, it amazes me—I'm not a short woman—but just looking up at you makes me feel dizzy.'

Hell, he felt dizzy just looking down at her. 'Would you believe you appear *small* to me?'

'Then I'll definitely stick to high heels,' she said.

He had a sudden vision of her walking up the Cunningham's staircase, with him admiring her legs. 'When you get to know me you'll realise I am scarable,' he said with a grin. 'Is that a word?'

'They let in new words every day.' They walked on. 'I know you worry about your brother. I know you're desperately unhappy beneath the dark Byronic façade.'

'*Please.*' So self-assured, he looked embarrassed.

She decided being able to embarrass him pleased her. 'Okay,' she scoffed. 'So there's too much romance about Byron for you. Do you know I actually cooked that special lunch for you today because you've lost weight even since we met.'

'Well fancy!' He gasped in mock surprise. 'You mean you've been studying me with those amazing blue eyes?'

'I figure if *you* can look, so can I,' she answered crisply. 'Why did you want me to walk with you? Any particular reason?'

'I'm certain you walk a lot faster than Chloe,' was his flippant response. 'Why? Did you have something better to do? Like spend more time with your stepmother and sister?'

'Your family's not everything it should be.' She struck back.

'Indeed it's not,' he agreed with a rasp in his voice. 'When you think about it, Allegra, the two of us have lived through a lot of stuff. Though I've never had the unfortunate experience of being burned by a bad marriage.'

'What about singed by a love affair that went wrong?' she asked with feigned sweetness.

He only smiled. 'Not yet.'

'Don't lay money on it not happening,' she said. 'Falling in love is a dangerous business.'

'And your love for your ex-husband wasn't unconditional?'

'You're making me angry, Rory,' she said. In fact he was making her heart pound.

'And I don't blame you. I apologise. You raise my blood pressure, too.'

They had reached his Toyota, now Rory opened the driver's door.

'Don't count on getting this place cheap, either,' she warned, conscious her body was throbbing in the oddest way.

'Then I'll blame you for pushing up the price.' He turned to fully face her.

They were so close, on a panicked reflex, Allegra stepped back, her heart almost leaping into her throat. It was her turn for embarrassment to wash over her.

'So long, Allegra,' he said, his eyes holding a wealth of mockery. He sketched a brief salute. 'I'll get back to you in a day or two.'

'You've made up your mind now,' She slammed his door shut, beating him to it.

He studied her through the open window. The sun was turning her glowing head to fire. 'Be sure of it,' he said.

CHAPTER FOUR

JAY paused for a minute to catch his breath. His arms were aching from thrashing through the lignum swamp. His khaki bush shirt was soaked with sweat, his jeans soaked with a green slime and swamp water up to the knees. He and a couple of the men had been hunting up a massive wild boar as big as a calf that kept threatening the herd. They had chased it into the deepest reaches of the swamp where a man on his own would find it very easy to get lost. The swamp was home to countless water birds and pelicans, but was spell-bound to the aborigines who shivering in fear, refused to go into it. Jay didn't altogether blame them. An unearthly yellow glow emanated from the place, seeping into the air. Rory, of course, afraid of nothing always said it was a sulphur spring. Whatever the eerie glow was, it was almost impossible to get into the swamp's deepest recesses without a machete. A good enough reason for the boar to make its home in the dense thickets, out of the path of danger where it could wallow to its heart's content in the mud.

It had made one last stand, its ugly head lowered for a final charge. It glared at them with its little reddened eyes, a ferocious looking animal, its coarse black bristles caked in mud and slime. Two powerful yellowish tusks protruded from its lower jaw, curving upwards in half circles. Sharp tusks that could easily disembowel a man or gore him to death. Spear carrying aborigines on the plain, would have charged the beast and killed it, a manoeuvre so dangerous it made Jay shudder just to think of it, though he knew boar hunting had been considered an exciting sport for hundreds of years. Jay got off a single clean shot to the boar's heart. Its bulk quivered for a moment on its short powerful legs, then it rolled over with a loud squelching sound into the foul smelling mud.

That exploit had taken them far afield and it was a long ride back before Jay reached the home compound.

He had truly believed he fully appreciated just how much hard yakka Rory put in, day in and day out—how much responsibility he assumed without saying a word. Rory had a natural affinity with animals; all sorts of animals from the wildest rogue brumby hell-bent on freedom to the most docile calf. Rory wouldn't have spent the best part of the afternoon tracking down that boar. He could read the signs as clearly as any aboriginal. Rory had only been gone a month and already he was sorely missed by all.

Jay missed him terribly. First as a brother and his best friend: then as a buffer between him and their father and thirdly as the cattleman, the Boss-man, who ran Turrawin. Rory was the Compton every last station employee deferred to and took orders from without complaint. Rory was a natural born leader. Such men didn't come along every day. Their father, Bernard, Jay had long since recognised, had little going for him these days but bluster and a whiplash tongue. With Rory gone there was animosity where there had never been before. Not only that, it was on the rise among the station staff. Not towards *him* personally—he got on well enough with everyone—but the whole situation. Not content with ordering Rory off the station, their father had let it be known Rory wasn't coming back. Further more Rory had been disinherited.

What that had achieved was nigh on catastrophic. It had bonded everyone against his father. While the men had greatly admired and respected Rory, working happily in the saddle for him from dawn to dusk, they were becoming discontented and occasionally rebellious under him. Okay they liked him—they even felt sorry for him having the father he did—but they didn't look to him as the boss.

He wasn't a cattleman, though God knows he'd

struggled to become one. The trouble was his heart wasn't in it and he wasn't half tough enough. He wasn't much good at giving orders, either, or even knowing what best to do in difficult situations when Rory, the man of action, had always come up with a solution right off the top of his head. Jay's only gift was fixing things, especially machinery. Rory had constantly reassured him that was a considerable gift. He could take any piece of faulty station machinery apart and put it together again in fine working order. Just like he had once longed to put the damaged human body back together.

He was thirty years of age, two years Rory's senior, but he still longed for the beautiful woman who had been his mother. She had understood him but she had never been strong enough to withstand their father. She was scared of him the same way Jay had been scared of him. The only one who wasn't scared was Rory. But even Rory had been known to flinch away from their father's vicious tongue.

Now that Rory was gone their father took it out on him.

He returned to the homestead at dusk, cursing the fact, as he did every day, his father was such a severe man who these days possessed not even a chink of lightness of soul. Bernard Compton had become damned impossible. When Jay entered the kitchen through the back door prior to taking a shower in the adjacent mudroom, he found his father slouched over the huge pine table, a whiskey bottle near his hand. Jay never remembered his father drinking so much but these past weeks he'd been getting into it as if alcohol took his mind off his troubles and what was already going wrong on the station. It was his grandfather and the Compton men before him to whom they owed the success of Turrawin. Then Rory. The necessary skills and attributes had skipped a generation. Oddly enough, his father, like him, was excellent with machinery but he took little pride in Jay's inherited ability. In fact he went out of his way to deride it.

'That's all you're bloody good for, son. Tinkering about!'

His tinkering had saved the station a lot of money.

Bernard Compton looked up as Jay entered the room. There was no welcoming smile on his heavy handsome face but a scowl. His once brilliant dark eyes were badly bloodshot. 'There's a couple of postcards from your brother,' he said, taking a gulp of his drink.

'You've read them?' Jay moved towards the table, feeling a rush of pleasure and relief at hearing from Rory again.

'Why not? They're bloody postcards aren't they?'

'They're addressed to me,' Jay pointed out quietly, picking them up. 'You shouldn't have sent Rory away, Dad. We can't do without him.'

'I'm not asking him to come back, if that's what you think.' Bernard Compton's face was set grimly. 'I don't get down on my knees to anyone least of all my own son. No respect, Rory. No respect at all. Looking at me with his mother's eyes.'

'Mum's beautiful eyes,' Jay said, his glance devouring what was written on the two postcards, each from different Outback towns. 'He's at a place called Jimboorie. Or he was.'

'I can read,' Bernard said roughly, staring up at his son. Jay was a handsome big fellow, strong and clever, but for God knows what reason glaringly inadequate when it came to running the station. 'So what do you want me to do about it?'

'Beg Rory to come home, Dad,' Jay answered promptly. 'The men look to Rory, not me.' *Not to you, either,* hung heavily in the air.

'He made his bed now he's got to lie in it,' Bernard Compton said. 'What we need is an overseer given you're so hopeless.'

'You're not much better,' Jay retorted, almost beyond caring what his father thought. 'Why didn't I have the guts to do what I always wanted to do?'

'Become a doctor?' Bernard snorted, and threw back the whiskey.

'I'd have been a good doctor,' Jay said in his quiet way. 'It's in my genes. I should have pushed for it.'

His father hooted. 'You've never pushed for anything in your life.'

Not with a father I hated and feared. 'Maybe there's still time to make plans,' Jay said. 'Rory told me there was.'

'That's because *he* wants Turrawin.' His father told him with a savage laugh. 'There's no end to your gullibility, son. Rory wants Turrawin,' Bernard repeated.

'Well, I don't want it, Dad,' Jay replied, his unhappiness growing more unbearable every day.

'Why, you gutless wonder! I'm ashamed of you, Jay,' Bernard Compton thundered, striking the table with his large fist.

'Do you think I don't know that?' Jay asked in a weary voice. 'You've bludgeoned me over the head with it for years, Dad. But my inadequacies are modest compared to yours. All you're good for is letting loose with the venom.'

'Why you—!' Bernard Compton, his face flushed a dark red, started to rise, but Jay, a powerful young man, shoved him back down on his chair. 'When I was a kid I used to find you very frightening. Mum did, too. But no more. I pity you from the bottom of my heart. You're a hollow man. Rory should have Turrawin. I'm the one who has to give up on this life I was never meant to lead.'

'What are you saying?' Bernard Compton's bloodshot eyes were filled with shock and disbelief.

'You heard me. Rory should have Turrawin otherwise this historic station will go steadily downhill. Only Rory can save it.'

'Over my dead body,' Bernard Compton exploded, glaring at his son.

'Why do you hate him so much?' Jay marvelled. 'He's your son, isn't he? Is there some bloody thing we don't know? Is that why Mum left? What's the goddamn mystery?'

Bernard Compton gave an awful grunt, clutching the whiskey bottle and pouring himself another double shot. 'Of course Rory is my son, you idiot. And I don't hate him. I bloody well admire him like I admired my old man. But there has to be a lot of space between us. I don't want him on my territory.'

'You're afraid of him aren't you? He's everything you wanted to be. Grandad loved him so much. He loved *me*, but I always knew Rory was the favourite.'

'That old bastard!' Bernard swore blearily. 'He certainly didn't love me. He always made me feel a fool.'

'Then I'm sorry, but it was never his intention. Grandad was a really good man. I'll stay with you, Dad, until we get a competent overseer in place. I thought we could bring Ted Warren in from Mariji. He's more competent than I am to handle things. Then I'm going to get a new life. Up until now I've always had the weird feeling I'm on hold with nothing to hope for. That has to change. But first, I'm going to find my brother.'

Allegra stood on the front verandah watching life giving rain pour down over the burdened eaves in silver curtains so heavy it was impossible to see out into the home gardens. It was well over a week now since Rory Compton had made the two-hour journey from Jimboorie township to Narooma with his offer; an offer Valerie and Chloe had near jumped at. She on the other hand had made it abundantly clear it wasn't enough, although she pretty well believed him when he said it was the best he could do. He didn't seem the man to try to beat them down. Clay Cunningham didn't think so, either. She'd already had a conversation with Clay, a man she trusted, who had revealed a little more about Rory Compton's situation. It was true his brother, Jay was to inherit historic Turrawin. True by all accounts—word in the far flung Outback flew around with astonishing speed—Bernard Compton had disinherited his younger son.

Rory Compton was no longer part of a wealthy family of pioneering cattle barons. Times for Rory had changed. He was out on his own albeit with the wherewithal to purchase a smallish run. Nothing that could possibly match what he had come from, but a property a man with his talents could build on and make prosper. Allegra was sure of it.

Rory Compton was a man of substance at twenty-eight. No great age. Her father would have judged him square in the mould of builder-expander. A man who exuded all the drive, ambition, know-how and ideas to turn middle of the road Naroom into a financial success. After that, she supposed, he would move on to bigger and better things. His offer had been basically, their reserve $3.5 million. She was sticking out for $4 million knowing despite depreciation and a big drop in stock numbers, Naroom was worth that. Or were her emotions too heavily involved? Naroom was her *home*.

The magic of the place! Yet she seemed to be the only one now her dad was gone to feel it. Anyway as far as borrowing went Rory Compton still had his name. A name to be reckoned with. His bank had approved his loan in what seemed to her record time. Her gut feeling was the bank could go $500,000 more.

No surprises a huge family fight had developed. Her on one side: Valerie and Chloe on the other. If she had ever thought and hoped there was some love between her and her half-sister she soon found out when the chips were down, there wasn't. Even thinking about the things Valerie and Chloe had said to her brought the sting of tears to her eyes. At one point she even thought Valerie would come at her in a rush of physical rage. Valerie was not to be thwarted. She wanted out like a wild horse wanted its freedom. And don't for the love of God get in the way. Whatever Valerie wanted, so did Chloe. The gang of two.

It wasn't as though she had been adamant with a no. Their combined clout equalled hers. All she wanted was a better offer. Or the opportunity at least to see if he could come up with a better offer? Surely that was reasonable? She was doing this for her dad, not for herself. His memory. Yet Valerie and Chloe had branded her with every unjust name they could think of.

'I'll tell you straight! I despise you for being so selfish!' Valerie had raged. 'Why did you come back here? We didn't want you.'

It doesn't take a lot of words to tear a heart out. What point in saying she had a perfect right to come back. Naroom was as much her home as theirs. More. But they obviously thought her marriage, however short, and their long tenancy downgraded her rights.

The following morning they left in a great flurry, catching a charter flight to Brisbane.

'I'm going to make it my business to consult with a top lawyer regarding *my* rights,' Valerie announced a half an hour before their departure. 'I was

Llew's wife! Surely to God I had the stronger claim? But no, I finished up with a mere quarter of everything.'

'A quarter of the estate amounts to quite a lot, Val.' Allegra tried to get a word in edgeways.

But Valerie wasn't prepared to listen. 'I'm going to see about contesting the will. It's an outrage your share was double mine. Anyone would side with me on that one. The *wife* should be the main beneficiary. I know you worked on your father. You kept at him and at him until he saw things your way.'

A wave of futility crested then crashed on Allegra. For her and Valerie to reconcile was unimaginable. 'That is patently untrue, Valerie. For your information Dad and I never ever discussed his will.'

'And who would believe you?' Valerie countered, her eyes flashing anger and disbelief. 'Anyway I can't stand around arguing with you. We have a plane to catch.'

'Good but before you go I want you to know I have no intention of holding up a sale if that's what you want. All I'm seeking is the best possible price we can get.'

'Just see you stick to that!' Valerie responded, her voice charged with venom.

There was, alas, little hope what was left of family could survive. Her father gone Allegra felt she was well and truly on her own.

* * *

By late morning the rain had ceased and the sun came out in all its glory, dispersing the clouds. Allegra took the opportunity of saddling up Cezar, her father's big handsome bay, and riding out to check on the herd. After one torrential downpour the creek that had been low for so long had risen a good metre, the surging brown water frothed with white. It coursed between its green banks, spewing up spray wherever it encountered boulders and rocks. She had already given the order to move the stock in case there were further downpours, which was a strong possibility. It was the monsoon season in the tropical North. Anything was possible; deep troughs, cyclones. The cattle were now grazing all over the flats on either side of the creek. They all knew what flash floods were like. They had all seen dead bloated cattle with terror carved into their faces. It was not a sight one forgot.

When she was satisfied everything was moving according to plan she rode back to the homestead, rejoicing in a world the rain had washed clean. She loved the air after the rain. She loved riding beneath the trees getting showered with water from the dripping branches. Everything about her, body and spirit, rejoiced in the great outdoors. For sure she had made a name for herself working as a fashion editor. She knew she was very good at her job. She had natural flair but she had always known where her heart was. It was the *land* that made her happy.

She was approaching the house when she saw with a flare of excitement as big as a bonfire: Rory Compton's Land Cruiser parked in the driveway. A moment later she saw his tall rangy figure walk down the front steps, making for his vehicle. Finding no one at home he was obviously leaving. That couldn't be allowed to happen. This man was too much on her mind.

Allegra urged the bay into a gallop.

He saw her coming. The bay she was riding was too big and most likely too strong for most women but she was handling it beautifully. She was wearing a cream slouch hat crammed down on her head, but her dark red hair was streaming beneath it like a pennant in the wind. He remembered what a beautiful natural rider his mother had been. How he had loved to watch her. He was painfully aware his love for the woman who had borne him wasn't buried so deep it couldn't resurface at some time. A tribute to motherhood he supposed.

He found he loved watching this woman, too. Allegra Hamilton was luring him like a moth drawn compulsively to a lamp. From out of nowhere she was all over his life. He was even starting to miss her when he didn't see her. He was even starting to imagine her there beside him. Hell, he wanted more of her. More of her company. The good Lord had either answered his prayers or sent him one heck of a problem.

She reined in a foot or two away from him, one hand tipping her hat the brim turned up on both sides, further back on her head. Her posture was proud and elegant. God, what's the matter with me? he thought

The answer came right away. You've fallen fathoms deep in love.

'What brings you here, Rory Compton?' Her eyes sparkled all over him, his face and his body, setting up a chain of spine tingles.

He damn nearly said, *you*. But no way could her feelings be as well developed as his. He made do with business. 'I've come with my final offer,' he explained.

'Ah, so you've got one?' She dismounted in one swift, graceful movement, swinging her long slender leg up and over the horse's back.

'That's some animal,' he said, running his eyes over the handsome beast.

'Cezar.' She patted the bay's neck affectionately. 'Cezar was my father's horse.'

'I should have known. He's too big and too powerful to be a woman's horse.'

'Are you saying I can't handle him?' She had to narrow her eyes against the glare.

He spread his hands. 'Never, my lady. It was a pleasure to watch you. You're a fine horsewoman.

My mother was, too.' He hadn't intended to mention his mother at all. It just happened.

Her beautiful face softened into tenderness. 'You miss her terribly, don't you?'

'Here, let me do that,' he said, ignoring her question because he was too moved by it, coming forward so he could remove the saddle from her heated horse.

'It's okay,' she said, turning her head. 'Here comes Wally. He'll take care of it.'

'Fine.' Rory watched as a wiry-looking lad of around sixteen—he vaguely recognised him— jogged towards them, coming from the direction of the stables. He had a big cheerful grin all over his face. 'Thought I saw you comin' back, Miss Allegra.'

'We both wanted that ride, Wally,' she said and handed him the reins. 'Look after him for me, would you? You remember Mr Compton?'

'Sure do!' The boy, part aboriginal, studied Rory with obvious liking. 'Gunna buy the place, boss?'

'Allow us to work that out, Wally, if you don't mind.' Allegra broke in, her tone mild.

'Sure, Miss Allegra.' Wally's grin stayed in place. He hadn't taken the slightest offence. He took the reins to lead Cezar away. 'Nice to see yah, Mr Compton.'

'So long, Wally.' Rory nodded casually. 'Be good now.'

'Come into the house,' Allegra said as she turned

to Rory, struck by the dramatic foil his light eyes, tanned skin and black hair presented. He was so handsome it seemed to her he radiated a spell. She just hoped she was keeping her powerful response underwraps. But surely no red-blooded woman could fail to be aroused by such stunning masculinity, or not enjoy his male beauty. Even after the traumas of her broken marriage she couldn't help but wonder what he would be like in bed.

Face it. She'd been spending too much time wondering. At a time when she should be standing back, taking stock of her life, a new relationship had been thrown open. What to do with it? Briskly she made towards the front steps.

'So where are Valerie and Chloe?' Rory asked, as they moved into the empty house. He would have a huge job in front of him keeping up the businesslike aura.

'They won't be back here until next week,' Allegra said, throwing her cream hat unerringly onto a peg.

He saluted her aim with a clap. 'Are they taking a short holiday?' he asked. He wouldn't cry buckets if they weren't coming back.

'You could say that.' She turned to face him, filled with something very like joy. Where was all this leading? She only knew it was going too fast.

'Would it be considered impolite to ask why?'

Rory stared back at her, drinking her in. She was wearing a mulberry coloured polo shirt over cream jodhpurs that showed off the slender length of her legs and her very neat butt. She didn't appear to be wearing any makeup at all. Just a touch of lipstick probably to protect her mouth, but her beauty was undiminished.

'You're loads better off not knowing!' Her answer was wry.

'Tell me. One would have to be massively insensitive not to pick up on the fact you women don't have a warm relationship.'

'Okay, we had an argument,' she confessed.

'I would never have guessed! It involved my offer and your decision not to accept it, of course.'

'Clairvoyant as well.' She turned to walk into the living room and he followed.

God, she could lead me anywhere, Rory thought, not altogether proud of the way he had fallen so easily for her. Did he actually *need* a mad passion? Surely he had decided he didn't. Yet he was thrilled and apprehensive at the same time. Their being alone together could only draw them closer. He already knew he was going to go along with it, even though he recognised she had the capacity to hurt him badly. This was a woman who would want to go back to her glamour job in the city. That was something to be feared.

You fool, Rory! This is getting altogether too serious.

He was getting right into the habit of communing with himself. Now he glanced around the comfortable living room. 'Family arguments are no fun.' Boy, didn't he have some experience!

'You can say that again,' she sighed. 'My family doesn't want me here anymore. That's it in a nutshell.'

'Okay let's sit down,' he said gently, seeing how much that hurt her.

'We're going to haggle?' She settled into an armchair indicating he take the one opposite.

'If you like. A cup of coffee would make me feel better.'

She sprang up as if remiss at not offering him one. 'Me, too!' She was becoming addicted to this man and in such a short while. Yet right from the beginning an intimacy had existed she had never shared with anyone else. Explain *that*? 'Come through to the kitchen,' she invited. 'We can haggle in there.'

It was a big kitchen but his presence filled it up. Allegra busied herself hunting out the coffee grinder then taking the beans from the refrigerator.

'I'll do that,' he offered, moving closer.

'Fine.' Even her pulses were doing an Irish reel. 'Count to twenty, that should do it.' She opened a cupboard and took out coffee cups and saucers, trying to tone herself down.

'The rain was wonderful,' he said when he finished grinding the beans and the kitchen was quiet again. 'I found myself standing out in it.'

'I can understand that.' She smiled. 'I did, too. I was purposely riding under the trees so I could get a shower from the wet branches. Do you think we'll get more? Rain is so very unpredictable.'

'Certain to,' he said.

'How do you know? Don't tell me it's your aching bones?'

'I can *feel* it. I can *smell* it,' he said. 'Besides the rain is coming down in bucket loads in the North. The last report I heard a cyclone was forming in the Coral Sea. That's all it will take. It's either flood or drought. If the cyclone develops and we get torrential rain, the Big Three—that's the Diamantina, the Georgina and the Cooper—will bring the floodwaters right down into our remote South-West corner. The Channel Country is one vast natural irrigation system as I'm sure you know. You've never been there?'

'I regret to say, no. I spent years at boarding school, then university, then I married. But I will get there one day.'

'It would be nice to take you,' he said. 'The whole region can flood without a drop of actual rain. Seen from the air it looks like the whole country is underwater.'

'Of course!' She looked across at him in quick realisation. 'You *would* see it from the air. You have your own plane on Turrawin?'

He nodded. 'A Beech Baron and a couple of Bell helicopters. We use the choppers a lot for mustering. We also use the services of an aerial mustering company from time to time. Choppers have revolutionised the whole business.'

'I can imagine, with those vast areas.' She stopped what she was doing to study him. 'But it can be dangerous? I've heard of many instances of fatal light aircraft and chopper crashes.'

'Very dangerous.' He shrugged the danger off. 'But it's our way of life, Allegra. We have to keep our fears under control.'

'That's pretty amazing,' she said dryly.

'When fatalities happen our vast community shares in the heartbreak. We're all in it together. I've been in ground searches and aerial searches in my time. We've had two major accidents in the last twelve years on Turrawin. One death I regret to say. A really good bloke, one of our regulars who could fly anything and land anywhere so no one worried about him for quite a while. The other was a crash landing, but mercifully the pilot walked away. I've had a close call myself. Once I came down in the middle of a big paperbark swamp. In the Territory I could have been taken by a croc, but we don't have any crocs in the desert. Well not anymore.' He smiled. 'Though you can see them in our aboriginal rock paintings.'

She stared back at him fascinated. 'You have cave paintings on Turrawin?'

'We don't advertise, but yes. Some of them are amazing. One cave in particular is guaranteed to make you believe in the Spirit Guardians. The hairs stand up on my forearms and I consider myself pretty cool.'

'You *are* cool.' She laughed. 'I'd love to see that cave myself.'

'I wish I could take you there.'

'That would be wonderful,' she admitted recklessly. 'We don't have anything like that around here.'

'I know.'

His mouth, quirked as it was now, was framed by the sexiest little brackets. She realised she watched for those moments. That was what falling in love was all about. It seemed that for her this was the classic coup de foudre. Which by no means guaranteed things were going to turn out fine she reminded herself. As for it happening at such a turning point in her life she was beyond thought.

'You're very passionate about your desert domain, aren't you?' She said, knowing he would be passionate about most things.

'Yes, ma'am.' His crystalline eyes looked right into hers. 'It's like no other place on earth and Jay and I have managed to see quite a few. Australia is the oldest continent on earth. I think that accounts for a lot of the extraordinary mystique. It's the time-lessness, the antiquity, the aboriginal feel, the power of the Dreamtime spirits. Then there's the colour of the place…the vivid contrast between the fiery red earth and the cloudless blue sky. Every country offers its great and its quiet wonders.

'I've stayed a few times with friends, another cattle family, who own and run a magnificent ranch in Colorado. They have the Rocky Mountains for a backdrop. It's like *wow*! Then we had a great trip to Argentina a couple of years back. Business and pleasure. A wonderfully colourful and exciting place. We loved it. We managed to get in a few games of polo while we were there. They're the greatest as I'm sure you know. We even got to fly over the Andes. I love flight. I love flying. Being up there in the wild blue yonder all on your lonesome. It's tremendous!'

'Then you're going to miss it, aren't you?' she said, getting a clear picture of him seated at the controls of a plane. 'Naroom doesn't run to light aircraft.'

He shrugged. 'Well you *are* much closer to civilisation. Turrawin on the other hand is right on the edge of the Simpson. The sand dunes there peak at around one hundred feet and they run for a couple of hundred kilometres unbroken the longest parallel sand dunes in the world. It's really eerie the way they bring to mind the inland sea of prehistory. I've stood on top of our most famous dune, Nappanerica—'

'The Big Red?' She smiled, glad she knew the answer.

'The very same. A Simpson traveller, Dennis Bartell named it. It's closer to one hundred fifty feet. The most amazing little wildflowers come out after a shower. Not the gigantic displays we get after flooding. But it's fascinating to study the little fellas up close. There are so many you can't move without crushing them underfoot, but then they release the most wonderful perfume. You think you've died and gone to Heaven.' He purposely didn't say he thought the fragrance akin to the fresh fragrance that came off her body.

'And after flooding?' she asked. 'I've seen marvellous photographic shots in calendars.'

'Allegra,' he said dryly, 'You have to see the real thing.' As he spoke he was imagining her with a diadem of yellow daisies around her head. As young boys he and Jay had fashioned them for their mother. 'After heavy rain, the desert flora has no equal,' he said with unmistakably nostalgia. 'The landscape is completely carpeted by pink, white and yellow paper daisies. It's like some great inland tide. They even sweep up to the stony hill country. Even the hills come alive with thousands of fluffy mulla mulla banners and waving lambs tails. So many varieties of desert peas come out, fuchsias and hibiscus, our exquisite desert rose. Nature's glory confronts you wherever you look.'

'It sounds wonderful,' she said, moved by the controlled emotion in his voice and face. Nostalgia was written all over him 'The central plains must seem pretty tame to you after your desert home?'

He raised both his wide shoulders in a shrug, but he didn't answer.

'Is there no hope of a reconciliation between you and your father?' she dared to ask the question.

His face angled away from her, looked grim. 'I need to get as far away from my father as is humanly possible.'

Good God as bad as that!' she said, pondering the no-holds-barred bitterness and hatreds in family life. 'It seems to me you're a son to be proud of.'

He looked up then to smile at her, the smile that was impossible to resist. 'Why thank you, Miss Allegra.'

'I'm not trying to butter you up,' she said, a shade tartly to counteract that sexual radiance. 'Just a simple statement of fact.' Belatedly she put the coffee on to perk. He was just so interesting to talk to she had forgotten all about it. 'Take a seat.'

He pulled out a chair, resting his strong tanned arms on the table. He was wearing a red T-shirt with his jeans, the fabric clinging to his wide shoulders and the taut muscular line of his torso. It was hard to look past his physical magnetism. In fact it was making her jumpy. So jumpy she felt if he touched her she would fall to pieces. Wisely she stayed on the opposite side of the table.

'So what have you got to tell me?'

He was as aware as she was of the glittering sexual tension that stretched between them, but he tried to play it cool as befitting a serious man. 'I can go a little higher with my bid.'

She raised an arched brow. 'How high is *a little*?'

He turned up his hands. 'We'll split it between $3.5 and $4 million. My final offer, Mrs Hamilton, is $3.75.'

'That *Mrs* Hamilton might cost you,' she said frostily.

'What did he do to you?' The intense desire to reach for her—the desire he was endeavouring to keep on simmer—damned nearly boiled over.

'What's made you change your mind about me?' she asked. 'When we first met it was like— What did she do to her poor husband?'

'I've had an epiphany,' he said, deciding there was safety in being flippant. 'For one thing, you're a great cook.'

'So the fact I can cook swung it?' The coffee was perking away merrily. She turned away to shift it off the heat.

'I'm joking!' There was amusement in his eyes.

'I know you are, Rory Compton,' she said tartly, betraying her stretched feelings. There was only one answer to all this. The question was when?

'So what *did* he do to you?' Rory repeated, his gaze very direct. He didn't think he could stop until he knew. That in itself was a danger.

She set his coffee down in front of him and pushed a plate of homemade biscuits his way. 'Isn't this too early in our relationship—for want of a better word—to ask a question like that?'

'One doesn't have to go together a long time to have a relationship.' He let his gaze rest on her. 'I thought we'd agreed we've well and truly bypassed the preliminaries?' He stirred three teaspoons of raw sugar into his black coffee.

'That's way too much sugar,' she murmured, unable to deny the truth of what he had just said.

'I take sugar to rally my flagging spirits. Not that I actually need it right now.' The little sexy quirks bracketed his mouth again. 'If you won't answer my question about your husband, answer this. What do you think of my offer?'

Her hand reached up to brush back a fallen thick coil of her hair. 'Well, I have to see what Valerie and Chloe think.'

'Stop being so damned evasive,' he said swiftly. 'Valerie and Chloe were ready to take $3.5 million.'

'Don't you dare look triumphant,' she warned him, seeing the silver glint in his eyes. 'I can't bear it!.' To her horror she felt tears swim into her own.

'Hey!' Rory reached across the table in consternation. He took hold of her satin smooth fingertips, curling his own work toughened hands around them.

Electricity pulsed the entire length of Allegra's body. She felt the shock of it as much as if he had taken hold of her and thrown her down on a bed.

'What's the matter?' Rory asked. 'Have I upset you? I didn't mean to. It's honestly all I can offer, Allegra.'

She blinked furiously. God, what was the matter with her? She was a quivering mass of nerve endings. 'I know that,' she said, looking down at their joined hands. She had never seen such a contrast in skin tones. 'You can let go of me now.'

'Fine.' He did so before he burst into flames. 'You've got skin like silk. It's your home is that it? In losing it to me you'd be cutting the last ties with your dad.'

'You're very perceptive,' she said shakily, convinced of it.

'Why else would you look so sad?'

The deep note of empathy, smote her heart. 'The grieving never ends, does it? It goes away for a little while then it comes back.'

'Old wounds never cease aching,' he agreed with

a philosophic shrug. 'Some people are far less able to cope with the pain than others.' He was thinking of Jay now.

'I don't have anyone anymore,' she said as though it had suddenly occurred to her. 'No father, no mother, no husband, no stepmother, no half sister. No *family*. At least you have your brother. Someone you know loves you and you love him back.'

His brooding expression was back in place. 'It's going to be damned difficult to see him if I can't set foot on Turrawin.'

'Your father must be a monster,' she exclaimed, leaning her head in her palm.

'Is that why you left your husband? *He* was a monster?' The fact he couldn't let the subject alone proved he was in over his head.

'He was a clown!' The words burst from Allegra before she could take them back. 'God that sounds awful. Forget I said it.'

He didn't speak for half a minute, he was so surprised. Clown? He hadn't been expecting that! 'So you don't hate him so much as despise him,' he asked, registering an involuntary wave of relief.

'Why are you so interested in my past life?' she asked.

He smiled. Tantalising. Heartbreaking. It seemed to her that smile was coming more frequently. 'You know why, even if I am trying to slow myself down.

I don't want to frighten you away, but you're the most romantic, the most glamorous woman I've ever met. And you smell like a million crushed wildflowers.'

Her heart faltered, plunged on. 'That's one sweet compliment for a cautious man, Rory Compton.'

'I just can't help myself. There's something so right about you, Allegra. Too much danger, too.'

'In what way?'

He looked past her. 'I'm an Outback cattleman. You're a woman with a glamorous career in Sydney.'

'So I am,' she said, suddenly plummeted into bleakness.

He wanted to pull her into his arms, stroke that melancholy expression away, instead he spoke bracingly, trying to keep both of them on an even keel. 'It was one hell of a trip around the property with Chloe. Her driving isn't so much dangerous as unlawful. What about the two of us riding out? I know you've still got some good horses.'

Instantly she felt a surge of pleasure that blew her troubles away. 'Great minds think alike! I was planning that myself. You can ride Cezar if you like?' She was aware of her desire to see him on horseback. She hadn't the slightest doubt he'd been a superlative rider.

His eyes widened for a second. 'I'd really appreciate that, Allegra,' he said. 'And I'm honoured. Cezar is a splendid animal.'

'You're welcome.'

'Great!' He stood up, cattleman coming to the fore. 'I hope you've had your men shift the cattle off the river flats. If there is more rain the water will rise above the escarpments of the creek. It will run a bumper and then, you'll have trouble on your hands.'

Allegra rolled her eyes heavenwards. 'Do you think I don't know? I'm not stupid, Rory Compton.'

'I'm starting to think you're a paragon,' he said dryly.

Allegra took the final gulp of her coffee.

'Right!' He pushed back his chair. 'Let's get going while the sun's out.'

CHAPTER FIVE

HE WAS already acting like Naroom was his own, Allegra thought, torn between acceptance and an understandable sense of loss. It was midafternoon, stiflingly hot and humid even though the sun had disappeared under a great pile-up of incandescent clouds. The smell of sulphur was in the air. It was as though one only had to strike a match for the whole world to go up in flames. Even the birds had stopped singing, lapsing into the silence that precedes a storm. Presently a wind sprang up, gaining velocity. Spiralling whirlwinds danced across the darkening landscape sending out their own clouds of dust, leaves and split, sunscorched grasses.

There was a lot of water stored in those ominous clouds. The rain couldn't have been more welcome but she dreaded the thought of hail. Many times in her life she'd seen it come down on Naroom with hellish fury, hailstones as big as cricket balls, bombarding the herd and sometimes killing the small game scurrying through the pastures.

Allegra roused herself from her thoughts. Rory hadn't been at all happy with the distance north of the homestead Gallagher and his off-sider Mick Evans had moved the cattle so he rode off with steely purpose to let them know. Allegra sat silently on her horse watching. There was always work to be done on a station; always another job.

Rory would get the men moving, she thought with satisfaction. It seemed only a man, a tough cattleman with a superior knowledge and experience of cattle could fill the shoes of Boss Man. Women need not apply. The outer areas of the run would be safe but he wanted *all* the cattle concentrated in the home pastures mustered and moved off the creek flats. One of the major problems with the station hands since her father's death, then the loss of their competent overseer—Valerie's disastrous decision—was that the men were sinking deeper and deeper into lethargy, understandably uncertain of their future when times weren't easy. Even the cook had taken off, but cooks were always guaranteed of a job.

Well, I gave them their orders, Allegra consoled herself. The *right* orders. 'Remember now. High out of the creek's reach!' It was clear they had only half done the job. She had fully intended to check on them. She knew she had to, but Rory's arrival had set her back. She watched him ride back to her, the stirring sight bringing the sting of tears to her eyes. Cezar was more than a touch temperamental but Rory wasn't having the slightest trouble making a near instant communication with her father's horse, essentially a one man horse although Cezar had gradually accepted her.

'You're not happy are you?' she asked, studying his expression as he reined in alongside.

'No, but there's no use worrying about it. We have to get cracking. We need to shift all the cows and calves on the other side across the creek.' There was a dark frown on his face. 'I've told those two layabouts if they're interested in holding on to a job they'd better shake themselves up. Big time. We'll never get the stock across if the creek starts flowing any faster. As it is we'll have to push them with stock whips. They're certain to be nervous, especially with this wind blowing up.' He glanced heavenward at the threatening sky. 'I've sent Gallagher to get the Jeep and bring it down here. Some of those calves are pretty small. They'll hold the rest up. We can pick 'em up and shove them in the back of the Jeep.'

'Right, boss!' She spoke in a voice of exaggerated respect.

'It needs to be done.' He gave her a querying look.

'Of course it does. Just having a little joke. I did tell them, you know.'

'Obviously they weren't paying the right amount of attention,' he said crisply. 'They will now. If you ride back to the stables you can tell young Wally we need a hand. On the double. Doesn't anyone use their own initiative? What about you?' He cast a dubious eye over her slender, ultrafeminine frame. 'I'll understand if you don't want to join in. It'll be hard work and we're pushed for time thanks to those two. We need them otherwise you should sack them on the spot.'

'They need sacking,' she agreed. 'And don't be ridiculous. Of course I'll help. That's what I'm here for.' She wheeled her horse's head about. 'They're all docile beasts on Naroom. We don't have your mighty herds to contend with. No rogues, no wild ones, no clean skins, either.'

'Off you go then,' he urged. 'We've got a lot to do before the weather worsens.'

A big storm broke around dusk but by then they had every last lowing beast up on high ground. Allegra's ears were ringing from the crack of the whips. They kept them sailing well above the backs of the herd while the loud sound drove them on. Darkness was closing in fast, the sun almost swallowed up. The familiar landscape was shrouded in a sodden mist that drenched them in seconds.

'Dig your heels in!' he called to her.

She didn't need to be told twice. The temperature had dropped considerably and she was shivering. When they arrived back at the homestead, the two of them ran quickly from the stables towards the rear entrance of the house. Once she went for a sickening skid, floundered wildly for a moment before he caught hold of her, amazingly surefooted in the quagmire.

At last they reached the back door, pushing it open and making for the mudroom cum first-aid room.

'While you take a shower I'll hunt you up some clothes,' Allegra told him, gasping from exertion 'That's if you don't mind wearing some of the clothes Mark left here? I was going to give them away. But so far I haven't got around to it.'

'Sentimental reasons?' He was busy pulling off his muddy boots.

'No,' she said shortly.

'I couldn't wear them otherwise.' Now he was stripping off his soaked T-shirt with total unselfconsciousness, throwing it in the tub before he turned back to her. His eyes blazed like diamonds in his dynamic face. His hair was like black silk. A beautiful man. 'Sure there's nothing of yours I could wear?' he joked, putting up both hands to skim back that wet hair.

Her heart skipped a beat and her blood coursed to her most sensitive places. She wasn't sure how she liked him best. Dressed or undressed? Hell, she couldn't just stand there admiring him, though she actually felt like taking the grand tour around him. Instead she managed a laugh. 'We're not really of a size. Don't worry, everything's clean. You can't imagine how fastidious Mark is. Most of the stuff is brand-new.'

'Beggars can't be choosers,' he said, running a careless hand over his wet chest, a gesture she found incredibly erotic.

'There are clean towels in the cupboard.' Never in her life had she drunk in the sight of a man's body like this. 'Everything you need is there. Don't get under the shower before I come back.'

'Why not?' He shot her a questioning glance..

'Naked men make me uncomfortable,' she joked.

He laughed aloud, looking wonderfully vital. 'Really? And you an ex-married woman! Surely you saw a naked man on a daily basis? Anyway there is such a thing as a towel. I assure you I'd have one at the ready. The last thing I want to do is throw you into a panic. I'll sit right here.' He turned, presenting the wide, gleaming fan of his tanned back and pulled up a chair. Then he sat on it, back to front, aiming his wonderful smile at her.

How had this man got so close to her? Why had she let him?

You didn't have a choice.

Yet he could cast her adrift. Anything was possible in life. But for now, he was making her feel things she had never felt before. She had to will herself to move. 'Won't be long.' She had already taken off her boots and used a towel to mop up the worst of the mud, now she padded towards the doorway leading into the hall. 'Not much chance of your driving back to Jimboorie.' She half turned back. 'Not in this!'

'So what are you saying, I can stay?' His tone was disturbingly mocking, even erotic.

She held his gaze as long as she could, shocked by the wrenching physical sensations in her body. She wasn't a schoolgirl with a crush on the captain of the football team. She was an experienced woman, twenty-seven years old. 'Well you're welcome to bolt if you think it's too risky,' she said tartly.

'Never!'

Rory offered up a silent prayer.

And lead me not into temptation.

'I'll stay,' he said. 'Thank you most kindly, Allegra. It'll give us the opportunity to have a good long chat.'

Rory washed out his gear and threw it in the dryer. Then he turned to examining Mark Hamilton's clothing most carefully. Everything Allegra had selected was brand-new and fine quality. He read the labels. From the dark blue polo shirt to the beige cotton trousers and the classy underpants. He tried to visualise Allegra's ex-husband. Couldn't. Chloe had called him a 'lovely guy' handsome and clever. Was he *all* of those things? Allegra in a driven moment had called him a clown! What did that mean exactly? A man forever playing innocuous but annoying practical jokes? A man not seriously minded enough for her? He had to be impaired in some way. He was a poor lover? He was a violent lover? Clown didn't sound violent. Who knew what went on inside a marriage anyway? Besides he couldn't trust Chloe. Chloe had made an art form out of putting down her exquisite sister.

Hamilton was a heavier build. And some inches shorter. The shirt was okay. He had to hitch up the trousers with his own belt. Rory was much leaner through the waist and hips. The length fell short but okay, who cared? She had even found him a pair of expensive leather loafers that fitted well enough. He took a look in the mirror, thrust back his damp hair and laughed. He had never worn a shirt of such a wondrous electric-blue.

'Gosh you look like someone famous!' Allegra swallowed when she caught sight of him.

'Don't say a rock star.' He grimaced. 'The blue makes me look swarthier than usual.' He glanced down at the shirt.

'Far from it. It's great. You're a good-looking guy, Compton.' She led the way into the kitchen. 'I could find you work tomorrow.'

'You surely can't mean as a male model?'

'You want to check out what they're earning,' she retorted. 'The guys who get to model here and overseas earn a fortune.'

'No, thanks. For better or worse I'm buying Naroom. All we need is the paperwork done.'

'And Valerie's and Chloe's okay,' she tacked on.

'Consider that a fait accompli.' He watched her take salad ingredients out of the crisper in the refrigerator. 'What are we having?'

'Something easy,' she said. 'Steak and salad and maybe some French fries. This afternoon was pretty strenuous.'

'I did warn you.' He let his gaze rest on her, feeling a surge of desire. She had teamed a delicate little lilac top, which looked like silk—he had a mad urge to feel it—with a flowing skirt. Her beautiful hair streamed over her shoulders and down her back, drying in long loose waves. There wouldn't be a man alive who wouldn't get a buzz from simply looking at her, he thought. She was just so effortlessly beautiful. Exclusive looking yet she had worked tirelessly that afternoon. Tirelessly and extremely well. This might be a woman who looked like an orchid but she didn't hesitate to pitch in. He found himself full of admiration for her. She was a woman of surprises.

'Valerie and Chloe were prepared to say yes to $3.5 million,' he reminded her, picking up the conversation. 'Thanks to you they get more.'

She took two prime T-bone steaks from the refrigerator and put them down on the counter before turning to him. Her expression was brushed with worry. 'Valerie said she was going to consult a solicitor with a view to contesting the will.'

'In what way?' He could see that upset her.

'Dad left me a half share of everything,' she said, 'whereas Valerie and Chloe had quarter shares.'

'Tough,' he said, thinking she didn't have a problem. 'I'm no lawyer but I'm willing to bet your father left his will airtight. Don't worry, Allegra. I'd say Valerie was trying to make you suffer. You can bet your life she's already been on to a solicitor who's told her she hasn't a chance in hell of contesting the will. You won't be embroiled in any lawsuit and this deal will go through more smoothly than you think.'

'I don't really want it to go through,' she confessed, leaning against the table.

'Which part of me don't you like?' He stared at her hard.

'This is *home*, Rory.' She met his challenging gaze. 'My father brought my mother here as a bride.

I was born here. Even when I was away from it I still *lived* here, if you know what I mean?'

'I surely do.' He thought she put it well.

'To be honest I'd like to die here.'

He stirred restlessly at that. 'Don't for God's sake talk about dying,' he said tersely. 'You've got a long life in front of you. Would you want to stay here and work it?'

'I *could* do it,' she said. 'I'd have to sack guys like Gallagher and Evans and hire some good men. Then I'd see if I could get our old overseer back.'

'Well, well, well,' he said. 'Like I said, you're a *most* surprising woman. But then I don't know a lot about women. I grew up mostly in an all male environment. Even so I'm sure you're very unusual. Do you have the money to buy your stepmother and Chloe out?'

She lowered her head, picked up a shiny red capsicum and set it down again 'No, unfortunately. I didn't take a penny off Mark.'

'You were entitled to.'

'No.' She shook her head. 'I didn't want to do anything like that. He didn't want to break up the marriage. *I* did.'

'So he was the innocent party?'

'No he wasn't, Rory Compton,' she said with sharp censure. '*I* was the innocent party but don't worry about it. I thought maybe I could borrow like you.'

'Really?' He sat back, his hands locked behind his head. 'You could try but maybe you wouldn't be so successful,' he warned her. 'You're a woman and you have no real hands on experience.'

'All right, I know that!' she said, giving in to irritation.

'And what about your big city job? I thought you intended going back to it? Surely you'd miss city life? I mean it couldn't be a more different world?'

'Rory, I love the land,' she told him passionately. 'I know it's a little unusual my making such a success of being a fashion editor, but that's only a little part of me. I doubt I would ever have left home had my mother lived. At the beginning living in the city was like living in a foreign country. After life on the land, I felt so hemmed in by all the tall buildings and so many people rushing about. All our space and freedom was lost to me. You should understand.'

'Of course I do.'

She nodded. 'It's not a nice thing to say, but Val drove me away. Val and Chloe to a certain extent. I was made to feel an outsider in my own home.'

'Have you a photograph of your mother?' he asked, sitting straight in his chair again.

She sighed deeply. 'Sure. Wait here.'

Rory rose and walked to the sink feeling vaguely stunned. The last thing he'd expected when they had first met, was such a glamorous young woman would want to live in isolation. In his experience it was men who did that sort of thing. Solitary men who had pioneered the vast interior before admitting women and children to their lives. He knew plenty of reclusives who could only live in the wilderness. Not that the central plains country was anything like wilderness but Naroom was isolated enough. God knows what she'd make of his desert home! Or what had been his desert home he thought with a stab of pain.

His mind wheeling off in several directions, he began to run some of the salad ingredients— tomatoes, cucumber, a bunch of radishes and some celery—under the tap. He could see the mixed salad greens had been prewashed. He felt like that steak. He hoped she had some good English mustard. He was hungry.

Allegra returned a few moments later, holding a large silver framed photograph to her heart.

He held out his hand. Ah, genetics! he thought, much struck by Allegra's striking resemblance to her mother. There were the purely cut features, the shape and set of the eyes, the chin held at a perfect right angle to the neck. There was the same flowing hair, the deep, loose waves. The photograph was black and white but he was certain the hair was the same shade as Allegra's. Even the expression was near identical. Confident, forward-looking, self-assured. Yet this woman had died so tragically young. What a waste!

'It would have been hard for your stepmother to be confronted every day by the image of the woman her husband truly loved?' he spoke musingly, finding it in his heart to pity Valerie.

'Hey, I was only *three* when Val became my stepmother,' Allegra pointed out.

'But the extraordinary resemblance was there. And each year you grew it became more pronounced. By the time you were in your teens you were a powerful rival. Or an ever present reminder if you like.'

She gave him a wounded look. 'Whose side are you on anyway?'

His expression softened. 'I'm sorry, Allegra. I can imagine what it was like for you. In my family Jay took after my father. Physically, that is. Jay is nothing like my father, thank God. I took after my mother. I have her eyes like you have your mother's eyes. Eyes tend to dominate a face. My father loved my mother. Or as much as he could love anyone. He sure doesn't love me. I was one terrible reminder she left him. I had to pay for my mother's unforgivable crime.'

'So there's a parallel?' she said more quietly.

'Oddly, yes. Both of us are outsiders.'

* * *

The wind and rain kicked up another notch during the night. He awoke to near perfect darkness. Amazingly he had slept. He never thought he would with Allegra sleeping down the hallway. They had talked until after midnight about their lives, their childhood, events that had shaped them, without her ever giving away the reason for abandoning her marriage. He really needed to know. It had become a burning question. Simply put, how could he truly understand until he knew? His mother's abandonment had played such a destructive role in his life he had a natural fear of handing over his heart to a woman who one day might cast him aside. God knows it happened.

Afterwards they had walked around the homestead together like an old married couple, checking all the doors and windows. Only the sexual tension both refused to let get out of bounds, betrayed them. Their hands had only to come into fleeting contact for Rory's hard muscled body to melt like hot wax. He wanted her. He wasn't such a fool he didn't know she wanted him. Sexual magnetism. Each was irresistibly drawn to the other, yet each was determined to keep control. Besides, there were dangers in acting on the most basic, powerful instinct.

* * *

Something had caused him to come awake. Some noise in the house. Downstairs. Maybe they should have made the French doors more secure by closing the exterior shutters? The verandah did, however, have a deep protective overhang. He stood up, pulling on his jeans, which he had removed from the dryer earlier in the night. He opened the bedroom door and looked down the corridor. All was quiet. Why wouldn't she be sleeping after such an exhausting afternoon? They had shared a bottle of red wine as well.

It turned out to be what he expected—one of the French doors in the living room. It was rattling loudly as the wind blew against it. He opened one side, latched in back, then stepped out onto the verandah, feeling the invigorating lash of the moisture laden wind. It felt marvellous! Rain to the man on the land was a miracle. The most precious commodity. In the Outback it was either drought or flood. He knew the creek would be in muddy flood by now. Thank God he'd arrived when he had. A woman no matter how willing to chip in wasn't meant to do backbreaking station work.

It took him only moments to secure the shutters, then the interior doors. One of the bolts on the door had worked its way loose, hence the rattle. He padded back into the entrance hall a little disoriented in a strange house. There was less illumination now that he had pulled the shutters. What he had to do was turn on a few lights before he blundered into something and woke Allegra. He didn't think he could cope with seeing her floating towards him on her beautiful high arched feet. He just might grab her, pick her up in his arms, and carry her upstairs…

'God!' He gave a startled oath as a wraithlike figure walked right into instead of through him. He held the apparition by its delicate shoulders.

'Allegra!' He sucked in his breath. Apparitions didn't have warm, satiny flesh.

'Who did you think it was, Chloe back home?' Her voice in the semidarkness came as a soft hiss.

'Out of the question. Chloe's shorter and a lot plumper than you.'

'Don't for God's sake ever call her plump to her face.'

'I wouldn't dream of it. I tried not to wake you.'

'When you were making so much noise?' Her voice rose.

'Pardon me, I was very quiet. Besides, what were trying to do to *me*? For a split second I thought you were a witch.' Very carefully he took his hands off her. Steady. Steady. He could smell her body scent like some powerful aphrodisiac.

'Witches don't flap around in nighties.'

He was seeing her more and more clearly. 'Are you mad? Of course they do. What's the matter anyway? You're as much out of breath as if you've been running.'

'I was trying to exercise caution as it happens,' she admonished him. 'You gave me a fright, too.'

'Then I'm sorry. There's nothing dangerous about me.'

She laughed shakily. What were they doing here, absorbed in a crazy conversation conducted in the near dark? 'I have news for you, Rory Compton.'

'Better not to tell me. It was one of the French doors. I've closed the shutters. I should have done it before.'

A shiver of excitement came into her voice. 'The wind is much stronger now.'

It couldn't be stronger than her magnetic pull. Rory marvelled at his self-control. Maybe honour could explain it? 'Why are you whispering?' he asked.

'I really don't know and I don't want to find out,' she whispered back. 'We should turn on a light.'

'Damn, why didn't I think of that?'

'The creek will have broken its banks.'

'Any chance of your speaking louder?'

'Oh, shut up!' The tension between then was electrifying. 'I'm *so* glad you were here, Rory!'

'*Am* here,' he corrected. 'Now, where the heck *is* the light switch for the stairs?' He knew it was dangerously wrong to keep standing there. Another minute and he'd reach for her. There was only one answer after that.

'I'll get it.' She slipped away like a shadow. Another second and lights bloomed over the stairs and along the upper hallway.

Behind him the tall grandfather clock chimed three.

'Ah, just as I thought!' he exclaimed. 'The witching hour!'

She was standing beneath a glowing wall sconce. It gilded the dark rose of the long hair that framed her face. He saw she was wearing a magical silk robe, a golden-green, with pink and cerise flowers all over it. It had fallen open down the front so he could see her nightgown, the same cerise of the flowers. It gleamed satin. So did the curves of her breasts revealed by the plunging V of the neckline. For a minute his strong legs felt like twigs.

Allegra drew her robe around her, scorchingly aware of his intimate appraisal. She was so aroused she was nearly on fire.

So why aren't you moving?

'We'd better go back to bed,' she said in another furious whisper. 'You go up.'

'Why not leave those two wall sconces on?' he suggested, not wanting and wanting so much to delay her. No words could describe how he felt. There was something magical about her. 'There'll be enough light to see us up the stairs.' He could only wonder at how composed he sounded when his body was flowing with sexual energy.

'The rain seems to be slowing.' She switched off the main lights, then padded on her slippered feet to the base of the stairs. 'Coming?'

He was awed by the electric jolt to his heart. 'Coming where?' He had a sudden overpowering urge to tell her how much he wanted her.

Only she cut him off. 'You *can't* come with *me*!' Her voice trembled. She didn't confess she was terribly tempted.

'I can't help wishing I could.' He stared back at her, hot with hunger. 'Don't be scared, Allegra. I would never offer you a moment's worry.'

She almost burst into tears she was feeling so frustrated. 'I'm not scared of you,' she said. 'I'm scared of me. Haven't we progressed far enough for one night?'

'Years have passed off in a matter of hours,' he said wryly. 'Even then you haven't answered the burning question.'

There was a breathless pause. 'Ask it quickly. I'm going up to bed.' She fixed her jewelled eyes on him.

'What was so wrong with your marriage you had to abandon it?'

She might have turned to marble. 'Don't go there, Rory,' she said.

'You have to get it out of your system.'

She shook her glowing head. 'Believe me, tonight's not the night. Good night, Rory!'

'What's left of it.' He shrugged. 'See you in the morning, Allegra. I'll be up early to check everything's okay.'

'Thank you.' She was already at the first landing, intent on getting to the safety of her bedroom and shutting temptation out. 'If you knock on my door, I'll join you.'

With that she fled.

CHAPTER SIX

THE rain stopped in the predawn .The air was so fresh it was like a liqueur to the lungs. The birds were calling ecstatically to one another secure in the knowledge there was plenty of water. In the orange-red flame of sunrise they drove around the property, Rory at the wheel of the Jeep, revelling in the miracles the rain could perform. Overnight the whole landscape had turned a verdant glowing green. Little purple wildflowers appeared out of nowhere, skittering across the top of the grasses. Hundreds of white capped mushrooms had sprung up beneath the trees that were sprouting tight bunches of edible berries.

They checked on the herd together. It had been little affected by the torrential downpour. The stock had come through the night unscathed and without event. The hail Allegra had feared had not eventuated. Cattle were spread out all over the sunlit ridges to the rear of the homestead. It was great to see them so healthy, their liver-red hides washed clean by the downpour.

The creek as expected had burst its banks. They stood at the top of the highest slope looking down at the racing torrent. It was running strongly, and noisily, carrying a lot of debris, fallen branches from the trees and vast clumps of water reeds torn up by the flow. When the water hit the big pearl-grey boulders the height reached by the flying spray was something to see. The area around the big rocks churned with swirling eddies of foaming water.

For a time neither of them spoke, simply enjoying the scene and the freshness and fragrance of the early morning. Both of them knew what this life-giving rain meant; how important it was to the entire region. A flight of galahs undulated overhead in a pink and magenta wave. Exquisite little finches were on the wing, brilliantly plumaged lorikeets chasing them out of their territory with weird squawks. Waterfowl, too, were in flight. They came in to the creek to investigate, fanning out over the stream. Allegra and Rory watched as the birds skimmed a few feet above the racing water, then collectively decided it was way too rough to land. They took off as a squadron, soaring steeply back into the sky again. Water was a magnet to birds. They would be back, from all points of the compass just waiting for the raging of the waters to slow and the creek to turn to a splendid landing field.

'Rain, the divine blessing!' Rory breathed as he watched the torrent downstream leap over a rock. 'No rain our way as yet.'

Our way! His beloved Channel Country. They had listened to the radio for news. The late cyclone that had been developing in the Coral Sea was now threatening the far North. Drought continued to reign in the great South-West.

'When it comes, the creeks, the gullies, the waterholes, the long curving billabongs will all fill up,' he continued in a quiet but compelling voice. 'The billabongs cover over with water lilies. None of your home garden stuff. Huge magnificent blooms. Pink, in one place, the sacred blue lotus in another, lovely creams, a deep pinkish red not unlike the colour of your hair. When the rains come the landscape just doesn't get a drenching, the vast flood plains go under.

'We've been totally isolated on Turrawin before today, surrounded on all sides by a marshy sea. When the storms come they come with a vengeance. It's all on a Wagnerian scale—massive thunderheads back lit by plunging spears of lightning. Getting struck and killed isn't uncommon. We had a neighbour killed in a violent electrical storm a few years back.'

Allegra turned to him, registering the homesickness on his handsome face. 'How are you going to be able to settle here, Rory, when your heart is clearly somewhere else?'

He adjusted his hat to further shade his eyes from a brilliant chink of sunlight that fell through the green canopy. 'I told you, Allegra, I can't go back. My home is lost to me.'

'You couldn't find a suitable property in your own region?'

He gave a humourless laugh. 'I could find one, maybe, but I couldn't pay for one. No way! We're talking two entirely different levels here. Our cattle stations—kingdoms are what they're called and it's not so fanciful—dwarf the runs in this area. I have to start more or less around the middle and work my way up.'

Her brows were a question mark. 'But are you going to be happy doing it?'

'Okay, I understand you.' He shrugged. 'The Channel Country is the place of *my* dreaming. It speaks to my soul like Naroom speaks to yours. This is beautiful country, don't get me wrong. Maybe it hasn't got the haunting quality of the desert, or its incredible charisma, but I'll settle here. I have to.'

'I don't think I'd count on it,' Allegra said, shrugging wryly. 'Your love for your desert home won't be shaken off any more than my father's love for my dead mother. Some loves go so deep nothing and no one can approach them.'

'Thinking twice about selling then?' he asked, filling his eyes with her. Her lissom body was clad in a navy and white top and close fitting jeans No makeup again, save for a pink gloss on her mouth. Her thick hair was woven into a rope like plait. He'd never seen a woman look better.

'Valerie and Chloe, when they return, will demand Naroom be sold,' she answered. 'I don't think we could ask for anyone better than you to take it on. You're an astute, ambitious man. I haven't the slightest doubt you'll make a big success of Naroom. And then you'll move on.' She spoke with a lowered head and saddened eyes.

'Hey, that's quite a few years down the line!' He tried to reassure her. 'But isn't that the way of it, Allegra? One expands, not stands still. Which doesn't mean to say Naroom couldn't and wouldn't remain a valuable link in a chain.'

'How good a cattleman is your brother?' she asked abruptly, moving a step nearer the top of the grassy slope to check it was a log that had smashed into one of the creek boulders and not a lost little calf.

'Jay got pushed into it,' he answered. 'He works as hard as any man. Harder, but—'

'He wasn't born to the job,' she cut in gently.

'I told you he wanted to be a doctor. It's a bit late but he could still be. I wouldn't know but he was a straight A student. Jay has a more sensitive side to him than I have.'

She gazed at him out of her black fringed eyes. 'I don't know if that's exactly right. I haven't had the pleasure of meeting Jay, but I would describe you as pretty deep, Rory Compton. You display your sensitivities in many ways.'

'As when?' he asked the question, then broke off abruptly, seized by a mild panic. 'Don't move,' he ordered. 'You could take a tumble.'

Even as he spoke the ground shifted beneath Allegra's feet. 'Oh…hell!' She threw out an arm. He grabbed it strongly, but the soles of her riding boots were slick with grass and mud. She slipped further down the bank with Rory straining to hold her. Allegra almost righted herself, about to thank him for his help, but in the next second a section of rain impacted earth gave way and the two of them began to roll over and over down the wet grassy slope, gathering momentum as they went. Their bodies crushed the multitude of unidentifiable little flowers that grew there in abundance, releasing a sweet musky smell.

Allegra, though powerfully shocked by their tumble, was experiencing a rush of emotions that included exhilaration and a blazing excitement. They were going to go into the stream. She knew that even if she couldn't look. It wouldn't be the first time she'd found herself in deep, fast running water. She was a strong swimmer. He would be, too. She didn't even have to consider it. His powerful arms were around her. What did she care if they had to fight the torrent? They were together. She felt like a woman is supposed to feel when she was with one particular man. A man who walked like he owned the earth.

Rory was taking the brunt of it, trying to protect her body from any hurt along the way. They were to an extent cushioned by the thick grasses that gave up a wonderfully pure, herbal aroma. As they careened towards the rushing creek he crushed her to him. He couldn't risk flinging out an arm. That meant taking one from her, but he was straining to gain purchase with his boots. Finally he hooked into something—a tight web of vines—that slowed their mad descent.

Another four feet and he was able to slam a brake on their rough tumble. They rolled in slow motion to a complete stop, finding they were almost at the bottom with the roar of the creek in their ears and the near overwhelming scent of crushed vegetation in their nostrils.

'Bloody hell, woman!' It was an eternity of seconds before Rory could speak. Then his words came out explosively. He was poised over her, staring down into her beautiful face vivid with exhilaration.

'Just hold it right there!' He held her captive, as if he believed her capable of jumping up and taking a header into the creek just for the hell of it!

She laughed with absolute delight. The sound was crystal clear. Transparent like an excited child's.

'Why did you stop us?' she wailed. 'I wanted to take a swim.'

'More likely bash your head against a rock,' he told her sternly.' The current is too strong.'

'Still I enjoyed it, didn't you?' She stared into his glittering eyes. 'I'll remember it for always.' The great thing was, she meant it. She raised her hand and very slowly caressed his bronze cheek, taking exquisite pleasure in the fine rasp of his beard on her skin. She fancied she saw little rays of light around his head. An energy that held her within his magnetic field?

'So what are you trying to do to me?' Rory stared down at her, equally bedazzled. 'What a repertoire of alluring little spells you have!'

'All called up with you in mind.'

'Then there's only one thing left to do.' The last tight coils of his self-control broke free. He was so hungry for her he didn't know how he was going to assuage it. He lowered his head, intent on capturing her mouth, only to see with a flame of wonder her lovely mouth ready itself to receive his.

What would he do to her if she let him?

He kissed her very slowly and gently at first until he had her whimpering and moving her head from side to side in agitation. Then his kisses strengthened in pressure and intensity as his passion for her surged. What a fool he was thinking he had schooled himself to restraint. The reality was he was so powerfully attracted to her he had lost the capacity for rational thought.

Time stopped. The whole world stopped. Pain and old grief were forgotten. His weight pinioned her body into the thick, verdant grasses.

'Am I hurting you?'

'Don't go way.' She loved the weight of him. Her eyelids fluttered shut and she caught the back of his neck with her hand.

He kissed her until both of them were gasping and out of breath. His hands were sliding slowly, sensuously, over her body as though learning it. Sometimes she led his touch, the delicate contours of her breasts swelling at his caress. Her heart felt like it was going to break out from behind her rib cage. Never before in her life had she felt such sensual excitement. Being with him had increased her every perception one hundredfold.

The breeze shook leaves from the trees. They flew down to them, golden-green, purple backed, landing gently in the glowing garnet coils of her hair. If ever a man could take a woman with his eyes he was guilty of taking her now Rory thought. In a minute she would lay her hand on his cheek again and tell him to stop.

Only she didn't.

For a woman who had lived three years in a bad marriage, Allegra felt unbelievably ecstatic. She wasn't unafraid of anything that was in him, because it was in *her*.

'Allegra, do you trust me?' His lips pressed against her throat.

'Do *you* trust *me*?'

Did he trust her siren song? The monumental shift in his line of defence couldn't have been more apparent. 'Do I trust life itself,' he murmured, continuing to trail passionate kisses across her face and throat. 'You must know I want you badly.' How could she not when she had been moving her hand over him as he moved his over her?

Allegra's breathing came fast and shallow. She *had* to tell him before his body took total control of his mind. 'It's not a safe time for me right now, Rory.' She tried to laugh, but couldn't bring it off.

'Oh my God!' He stopped kissing her, his sigh deep and tortured. 'Oh God, Allegra!' Frustration whirled through him with the force of a tornado. 'I'd better let go of you,' he groaned.

'Maybe you'd better.' Her own burning desire was at war with all ideas of caution and common sense.

She was panicked by the thought that desire for him could very well win if they didn't move. 'I didn't know all this was going to happen so soon.'

'Hell, don't apologise,' he said, his body racked by painful little stabs. 'So you could fall pregnant?' He helped her to sit up.

'It's a strong possibility.' She held a hand over her heart, trying to quiet her breathing.

'I wish to God I'd brought some protection.' His handsome face was taut with frustration.

'So do I.' She laughed without humour, her creamy skin covered in a fine dew of heat.

'I'm so desperate to get close to you,' he admitted, teetering on the edge of saying a whole lot more.

'Are you?' She turned to stare into his eyes, conscious of a sudden joy.

'You know I am. Damn, damn, damn,' he groaned. 'So what do we do? Let the flames die?'

'It might be a good idea.' She didn't bother to hide her regret.

'Would you *want* to have my baby?' he asked very quietly.

'Are you speaking seriously?' It wouldn't be the end of the world if she fell pregnant to him. It would be thrilling.

'Yes,' he said.

'What's going on in your mind, Rory?' She was trying to read it from his expression.

'You haven't answered the question.'

'I want children,' she said. 'I've told you that before.'

He took her hand, looking intently into her eyes. 'Do you think we have enough going for us to consider marriage?' He knew he was being carried to extremes, but maybe extremism was his natural bent? Either that or he had finally found his life's focus.

'Rory!' Allegra began to laugh a little wildly. For a minute she felt like she was flying; caught up by a great wind. She who had come through a catastrophic relationship was being asked to consider marriage again. What was even more astounding was she knew right away what her decision would be. Something extraordinary had happened to her. She had to seize the day.

'Well?' He took her chin, sparkles of light in his eyes.

'You don't have to propose to me to get me into bed,' she said, pierced by the look in his eyes. She was long used to men regarding her but this was something entirely different.

'You think I don't know that?' he said gently. 'I know this has come at an odd time, but can't you see the beauty of it? I want a family. So do you. We're much the same age. Neither of us is content to let things go on much longer. If I've shocked you with my audacity, perhaps you can think of it as a contract that could work extremely well for both of us as we both have the same aims. You wouldn't have to leave the home you love. You'd gain a half share as my wife and partner. You'd be able to hold onto your own money. It's important for a woman to feel financially independent.'

The words were business-like, but the warmth of real emotion was in the sound. 'I should say you're crazy!' Allegra was still flying high. To share a dream! Isn't that what she had always wanted?

'You know I'm not.'

'So what are you leading us into?' she asked as calmly as she could.

'Why a marriage of convenience for two people who just so happen to suit one another right down to the ground.'

'We can't have love, too?'

For answer, he turned her face to him and dropped a brief, ravishing kiss on her mouth. 'Wouldn't you say we're more than halfway there?'

So there was one secret between them. She was already there. 'Maybe we should slow down instead of full steam ahead?' she suggested before binding him to her.

'I'm going to leave that up to you, Allegra,' he said. '*I* won't change my mind. You're the woman I want.'

She kept her eyes lowered. 'You can't have forgotten both of us have a lot of old issues to work through?'

'We can work through them together.' His response was swift and sure. 'Have I dared too much too soon?' He searched her eyes for any hint of misgiving. 'I hadn't planned any of it. It took a tumble down the hill to shake it out of me. Love is a big word. Maybe the biggest in the dictionary. I don't think we're going to have a problem getting into bed together, do you?' he asked dryly.

No problem at all but she had to remind him. 'There's a bit more to marriage than sex, Rory.'

He nearly said what was flooding his mind. *I love you.* But the last thing he wanted was to frighten her off. 'Do you think I don't know that? We really *like* each other, though, don't we? Not that I'm about to knock great sex. Marriage would be very sad without it. But we have a lot in common. All the things we talked about last night. Our love of the land. Don't let any bad experience you may have had with your husband warp you.'

She felt a frisson of shock. She had never said a word to him about Mark. What then had he assumed? 'So much depends on our mutual love of the land, doesn't it?' she said, ignoring the reference to Mark.

'I'd be lying if I didn't say it was a crucial factor.' He didn't drop his gaze. 'I couldn't consider marrying a woman—no matter how much I wanted her—if I knew she might go off and leave me when the going got rough. Worse, leave our kids. You were being entirely truthful when you said the land is where you belong?'

'Of course! How could you doubt me?' She shook her head vigorously. 'I have my own dreaming.'

'Well then, it's a brilliant idea,' he said as though that clinched it.

'More like explosive!' Allegra knew she ought to be filled with doubts but incredibly she wasn't. She felt more like a woman who had been blind all her life then finally opened her eyes. In fact, she had never felt so good. 'You've got to give me a little time to think,' she said, paying a moment's homage to caution. Impossible to *think* when he was holding her hand and making love to her with his eyes. 'This is scary. Or it darn well ought to be. I didn't do too brilliantly the last time.'

'And you won't let me hear the problem. He didn't abuse you, did he?' Rory couldn't abide the thought. 'I'd go find him and horse whip him if he did.'

'And wind up inside a jail? I wouldn't like that. Mark isn't a violent man. In many respects he's the perfect gentleman. Everyone thought so anyway. People can act perfectly civilised but one barely has to scratch the surface to discover they're something quite different underneath. My dad didn't take to Mark. I knew that although Dad never put his concerns into words.'

'I'm listening,' he prompted, feeling an iron determination to protect her.

She bent her head, unsure how much to say. 'Mark was into a fantasy life. A *sexual* fantasy life.'

'One that bothered you?' he frowned.

'Once I found out he'd been unfaithful the marriage was as good as over. I hate to talk about it, actually. I forgave him the first time. I thought it was a one-off aberration and I felt badly about calling it quits so early in the marriage. But it wasn't. Mark continued his brief encounters with married women in our own circle. They made an absolute fool out of me. Opportunity is always present if one is looking for it.'

'Good God!' Rory made a deep, growling sound in his throat. 'He sounds like an oversexed adolescent.'

Allegra's shrug was cynical. 'A lot of men of all ages fit that description. Men and woman have affairs. Married or not. I saw a lot of it. One can't help attraction. The possibility is always there. If one is married the right decision is to consciously turn away from temptation. Some don't.'

'You never thought to get even?' he asked. 'Sorry, I withdraw that. I know you didn't.'

'You're dead right. I respected my marriage vows. I respected myself. That's why I had to get out.' She steadied herself to look into his eyes. 'I liked the way you checked the minute I said it wasn't the right time to have sex.'

'Why of course! You surely didn't think I would force the issue?'

'I didn't, but I *was* responding an awful lot. In a way it was a crisis and you dealt with it the way it had to be. Mark messed me up for a while. He's quite a bit older. Nearly ten years. He set out to mould me to *his* ways but he failed. He actually believed his little affairs were harmless. He swore over and over he loved only me. I was his *wife*. That put me on a pedestal instead of exposing me to ridicule. He swore he'd get help.'

'And did he?' Rory was having difficulty understanding a man like Mark Hamilton.

'I didn't wait around to find out,' Allegra replied flatly. 'I believed I did at the time, but I didn't love Mark. He was more a replacement father figure. Had I really loved him I'd have been devastated at the divorce, instead of just plain *mad* at myself. The state of my home life—the way I grew up—pushed me into trying to find someone safe. Mark had every outward appearance of being safe, except he wasn't safe at all. I made one hell of a mistake. I can't possibly make another.' She was too close to tears to say another word.

He drew her within the haven of his arm.' Did you tell your stepmother and Chloe about this?'

She nodded. 'But not all that much. They thought the world of Mark. In their eyes if anyone was to blame for the breakdown of our marriage it was me. Val has been compelled to find fault with me since I was a kid. I couldn't do a thing right. She used to make up stories for Chloe to believe and Chloe did. I used to be devastated. Not anymore. Over the years, Val has brainwashed my sister. Chloe would be a much better person away from her mother. In her heart Chloe knows it. Anyway there's nothing I can do there. It's all too late. There's a lot of deep resentment. Not love.'

'Was there *any* happiness in your marriage?' he asked.

'I can remember some good times,' she said. 'At the beginning.'

'Then let me make up for all you've missed.' His hand slid to her nape, cradling her head. He allowed himself the sheer bliss of kissing her again, only breaking it by force of will. 'You'll have to be really, *really* patient for the rest.' Mockery sparkled in his eyes.

'I guess I have to be okay with that.' Her voice was soft. He had taken her breath. Sunlight was filtering through the trees, warming them in its streams of golden light.

'I suppose we could live together first like couples do these days?' He put forward the idea as a way of giving her an option. 'Does that appeal to you? A trial run? We could take it in stages if that would make you feel easier in your mind. You can have all the time you want to get used to me. The same goes for me.' He gave a sardonic ripple of laughter. 'Although I'll never get used to you if I live a hundred years.' She had stopped him in his tracks when he had first laid eyes on her. She was even more beautiful to him now.

'You'll make some woman a terrific husband, Rory Compton,' she told him, thus stating her clear preference.

'Then that woman better be *you*!'

CHAPTER SEVEN

VALERIE'S face was a study. She jumped to her feet, moving towards Allegra as though she would like to slap her. 'How long now is it since your divorce and you're planning to *remarry*?' Her voice rang so loudly it bounced off the walls. 'Even knowing you the way I do, I can scarcely believe it.'

Chloe sat trembling, on the verge of tears. 'What did you *do* when we were away?' she demanded to know, her voice sounding thick in a clogged throat.

'Do?' Allegra repeated. She fell back from the kitchen table, as ever feeling outnumbered. 'I hardly think it's got a damned thing to do with you, Chloe. You should be thrilled I managed to get extra for Naroom, instead of questioning me like this. I haven't heard a word about the better offer.'

'Did you sleep with him?' Valerie threw out an arm so precipitously she knocked over a glass on the sink. It smashed on the terracotta tiles but all three women ignored it.

Allegra sat there wondering why after all these years, she was still stunned by their reactions. 'That's absolutely none of your business.'

A dark look crossed Valerie's face and her jaw set hard. 'I bet you did. 'You take no notice of the conventions. Mark was too much the gentleman to say a word against you.'

'Mark was no gentleman,' Allegra said, sick to death of the way they defended him. 'A gentleman is a man of decency.'

'And Mark wasn't?' Chloe's *pretty* mouth twisted bitterly.

Her tone struck Allegra as odd. So odd, she thought suddenly of those old photographs. '*You* didn't by any chance sleep with him?' Allegra's voice was so tight it was devoid of expression.

Chloe flushed a deep scarlet, then swiftly turned her head away, the very picture of guilt, colour flooding her face.

'What a criminal thing to say. Apologise now.' Valerie was breathing hard, her eyes fixed on Allegra and not her daughter. 'You're beautiful to look at, but you're not beautiful inside. That's the paradox with women like you. Apologise to your sister.'

Allegra ignored her, studying her half sister with contemptuous eyes. '*Did* you, Chloe? I always had a sneaking suspicion you did.'.

'Are you quite m-mad!' Valerie stuttered, looking like she thought Allegra beyond the pail.

'You, Val, are a fool.' Allegra spoke without looking at the woman. 'So am I for that matter. You *did* didn't you, Chloe. You did it as much to spite me as surrendering to Mark's charms.'

Valerie, openly incredulous, shook her head, but Chloe, unable to disguise her guilt but without a glimmer of remorse, put her face down into her hands and promptly burst into floods of tears as her only way out.

'Found out at long last!' Allegra said quietly, feeling sick to the stomach. 'What a hypocrite you are, Chloe. Always playing the role of Goody Two-shoes while you betrayed me in my own house.'

Chloe adopted a victim's expression. 'He wanted me. He waited for me.' She lifted her tearstained face to steal a look at her mother.

'The *bastard*!' Valerie erupted predictably. Nevertheless she took Chloe's shoulder in a hard grip. 'Sit up straight. You're always slouching about. You slept with your sister's *husband*?' She gave her daughter a look of the utmost reproach.

'Like I wanted to? He was after me. Anyway, what does it matter?' Chloe moaned. 'I was nothing to him. The only one who was ever important to Mark was Allegra.'

'And to think I've been defending him!' Shock

was written all over Valerie. 'You've got a hell of a lot of explaining to do, young lady.' She stared down at her daughter's mock penitent head. All Chloe was sorry about was she had been exposed. 'What was in your mind to do such a thing?' Valerie demanded to know.

'I don't really have an excuse. He took advantage of me. I'm sorry,' Chloe mumbled, managing to sound shattered, which in a way she was.

'Sorry? Is that the best you can do?' Valerie was suddenly seeing her daughter very differently.

Allegra just stood there, her head spinning. 'Only Dad saw through Mark,' she said. 'But Dad unfortunately held back because he thought I loved him.'

'Which you never did.' Valerie reverted to making Allegra the scapegoat. 'You just needed a stepping stone.'

'You saw that, did you?'

Valerie smiled grimly, but didn't answer.

'Not loving Mark isn't something I'm proud of, Val. I *thought* I loved him at the time. In retrospect it's pathetically clear I really wanted a home of my own. Someone to love *me*.'

Valerie turned away to sweep up the fragments of the broken glass. 'What a swine he was! He seduced my Chloe.'

'Don't believe it!' Allegra scoffed. 'Chloe was right there in the middle of it, ready to take whatever was going. I don't think I want to talk to you again, Chloe,' she said. 'Not after today.'

'Who would care!' Chloe shouted. 'All you do is *burn* people. Now it's Rory Compton who has to pay for coming into your orbit. You seduced *him*. I haven't the slightest doubt of that. You have seduction down to perfection.'

'My dear, I could take lessons off you,' Allegra said.

'What *did* happen with Rory Compton,' Valerie asked. her tone condemnatory.

Allegra studied her. 'Nothing as if you have any right to know. Rory came with a second offer, just as I told you. He had no idea you were away. He was enormously helpful shifting the stock to high ground. The creek was running a bumper. It's still high if you want to take the time to go down and look. He had to stay the night. It was raining far too heavily for him to drive back to Jimboorie.'

'And you lured him into your bed,' Chloe hit back. 'That's unforgivable, Allegra. You've always done it. As soon as any guy takes a liking to me you *have* to take him off me.'

'Haven't I told you that all along.' Valerie gave Allegra a venomous look. 'What are people going to say? Think of the scandal and so soon after your father's death. Let alone your divorce. But you scarcely care about that. You don't even know this man. You could destroy him.'

Allegra lowered her head in resignation. 'Val, you should have sought help a long time ago. The animosity that's in you is corrosive to the soul. I'll go back to Sydney until Naroom is sold. I can't stay here the situation being what it is. It's a thirty-day unconditional contract. Rory already has bank approval.'

'I want you to leave tomorrow,' Valerie said, slamming her two palms flat on the table.

'To hell with you and what you want. You forget yourself, Valerie. I'll leave when I'm good and ready.' Allegra's voice was so authoritative Valerie backed off. 'I'd be grateful if you could keep a civil tongue in your head until then. I've put up with your viciousness until now, but no more!'

'Viciousness?' Chloe jumped in to champion her mother.

'It's about time you stopped playing the ingénue, Chloe,' Allegra said . 'You're much too old for it. In your heart you know the situation. Your mother hates me.'

'Mum doesn't hate anyone,' Chloe declared, mostly because she needed her mother on side. 'I know she can be a little sharp tongued from time to time, but she doesn't *hate* you, Allegra. *I* don't hate you. But you've never let me shine. Can you understand what that does to me? I've always been overshadowed. You're the beautiful sister, the clever sister, the one people ask after. They come up to me and say, 'How's your beautiful sister?' I hate it.' Her blue eyes flashed anger. 'That's why I slept with Mark. To get back at you. I hated myself afterwards. I had to pretend it never happened to live. It was only the once anyway.' That at least was the truth. 'I didn't like it. Rory is different. He would have liked me if you hadn't been around.'

'Wishful thinking, my dear,' Allegra said disdainfully, and walked away from them without a qualm.

Allegra shocked a lot of people when she handed in her resignation.

'But you had such a future with us, Allegra,' Juleanne Spencer, the Editor-in-Chief and something of a national icon, told her, staring in dismay across her magnificent antique desk. Their meeting had already lasted forty minutes but Juleanne, who had great persuasive powers, was distressed she wasn't about to sway her clever and, she would have thought, highly ambitious Fashion Editor. Allegra Hamilton had *real* style and an uncanny ability to combine glamour, excitement *and* wearability into the beautiful and imaginative fashion shoots the magazine was famous for.

'How our best laid plans go astray!' Juleanne lamented, taking a moment to think back over at least a hundred cock-ups. 'Really, darling, the sky was the limit! You had mountains to climb. It might seem impossible now but one day I have to retire.'

'When you're so young!' Allegra exclaimed.

'Young at heart, dear. You know I won't see sixty again.' Juleanne when last she looked had her sixty-sixth coming up, but then she didn't do the normal calculations like everyone else. 'We were actually counting the days until you returned. You're valued around here.'

'Emma is well able to take over from me.' She spoke confidently, referring to her Associate Fashion Editor. 'She's doing it already. I've seen this month's magazine.'

'Emma's good, but she's not *brilliant*.' Juleanne wrung her heavily bejewelled hands, nothing under four carats in sight. 'What about if I offered you a hefty raise?' Money always worked. At least on most people.

'You've already offered a hefty raise, Jules.'

'It's a man isn't it?' Juleanne, three times married, moaned, as if all one could expect from a man once married was mental cruelty or physical abuse. 'One of those—are there any others?—who doesn't want you to have a career?'

Allegra sweetened her answer with a smile. 'I've really enjoyed my time with the magazine, Jules. I've loved working under you. You've been my in-spiration. I've turned myself inside out for you.

You're a living legend. But I find at the end of the day I'm a country girl through and through.'

'But darling, you don't *look* it,' Juleanne said in horrified amazement. 'You always look sensational. Which is really lovely to have around the place. I just can't see you down on the farm mulling around three million cattle, or is it sheep?'

'More like eight thousand cattle these days, Jules. We're understocked. That means more feed in times of drought. The Outback is where I was raised.'

'You can't take an extended leave and get it out of your system?' Juleanne suggested hopefully.

'No.' Allegra shook her head.

'So you're seriously considering life on the land?' Wonderment was all over Juleanne's marvellously preserved, un-Botoxed face. 'It's a man, isn't it?' she repeated her question. 'Of course it is,' she said sadly, accepting defeat. 'My advice is have an affair with him, darling. You have no idea how marriage can disrupt a good relationship. By the way, now you're well shot of him, I never did like Mark. He reminded me of my second. Kept telling me he loved me then tried to drown me in the hot tub.'

The day after settlement day Rory made another long journey to Naroom to say goodbye to Valerie and Chloe who were taking a long overseas trip with the proceeds of the sale. They were now very comfortably off but they stopped well short of being happy. In fact both mother and daughter were acting like there was no justice left in the world. The greatest offence that was offered appeared to be the fact he *and* Allegra were co-owners of Naroom. Then there was their decision to marry. It was greeted as being on a par with a heinous crime.

He knew Chloe had a minor crush on him—he was sure it would soon pass, and he was sensitive to her hurt, but he hadn't given her the slightest encouragement. Somehow she had convinced herself Allegra had deliberately ruined her chances. Both Chloe and her mother were eaten up by jealousy, using it as a justification for attacking Allegra whenever they could. No wonder Allegra had returned to Sydney until the deal was done.

Unmoved by his every argument, she had insisted on paying for her half share of the station. 'This is the way I want it, Rory,' she told him. 'There's no other way. If you want me, you'll agree.'

'It's blackmail,' he'd said.

'Does it matter? This is what I want. Our arrangement will work better if we're equal partners. I don't want you working yourself to exhaustion trying to pay off the loan quickly. Which is exactly what you'd do. This way money is freed up for other things. Buying more stock, for one.'

Well he had said it was an arrangement to suit

both of them. Allegra got her way. He was missing her so much his escalating emotions had firmed into an iron determination to take a trip to Sydney and bring her home.

Brilliant sunshine outdoors. A chill inside the homestead.

'I just hope you know what you're doing, Rory,' Valerie said, in the chastising voice she thought she had a right to. Valerie was big on rights. 'You haven't had time to get to know Allegra.'

'Oh, I think I know enough, Mrs. Sanders,' Rory replied, keeping a tight rein on his temper. What an awful woman! Not awful exactly. Totally obnoxious. Llew Sanders had made a huge tactical error there. Or maybe Valerie had kept her true nature underwraps.

Now she looked back at him with bitter eyes. 'Aren't you just the least bit apprehensive, considering Allegra couldn't make a go of her marriage?'

'I believe she told you why,' Rory spoke crisply. 'That good man was unfaithful.'

'Perhaps she drove him to it?' Like the leopard Valerie couldn't change her spots.

'I warned you about Allegra, Rory, but you wouldn't listen,' Chloe, the two-faced deceiver added.

'I believe I'm a much better judge of character than you, Chloe,' he said firmly. 'I can appreciate you've suffered believing yourself outshone by

Allegra, but that was hardly her fault. Happiness mightn't have eluded you if you hadn't been so jealous of your half sister.' He held up his hand as she opened her mouth to defend herself. 'No, let me finish. I can't sit here and allow either of you to attack Allegra. You do it all the time. It's upsetting. Worse, it's dead boring. I have an older brother, Jay. I love him very much. *He* will inherit Turrawin, when my father dies. Not me. If I'd allowed myself to become bitter about it, it would have ruined a wonderful relationship. There was nothing either of us could do. That was the way of it with you. Allegra could have been your closest friend, Chloe. Instead something bad happened. Between you and your mother, you turned her into an outsider.'

Valerie sat motionless, but the steam of outrage was rising off her. 'How dare you talk to me like that.'

'I do dare, Mrs Sanders.' Rory unfolded himself to his impressive height. 'If there's something I can do for you to help you get away, I'm happy to do it. Otherwise I'll go.'

'I prefer you did,' Valerie said very coldly.

It was futile to remain a moment longer; or point out the irony of being ordered off what was now *his* and Allegra's property. Rory didn't like to tangle with irate, irrational women. He walked down the front steps, making for his vehicle which he'd parked in the shade of a stand of gums. The trees were bearing enormous quantities of yellow blossoms enticing lorikeets in their dozens to feed noisily on the nectar.

He was surprised when Chloe came running after him.

'Rory, please stop,' she called.

It would have been churlish for him not to, but he was fed up. 'What is it, Chloe?' He waited for her to come up to him. A short run yet she was puffing hard. He suddenly saw it through Allegra's eyes. Chloe, the girl, always making excuses to stay at home with her mother. Chloe not getting outdoors and not getting enough exercise.

'I apologise for Mum's talking like that,' she said, darting a swift glance at his stern expression and away again. 'You must understand she's terribly upset.'

'I'm upset, too, Chloe.'

'She was only trying to help you!' Chloe sought to appease him. 'We've been through so much with Allegra.'

His expression was openly condemning. 'You ought to stop telling howlers, Chloe. It's a hard habit to break. Actually what Allegra's been through springs more easily to mind. But you can't help yourself, can you? It's almost become second nature. It seems to me, your mother has used you to bolster her position in the household. Personally I think she must have given Allegra one hell of a time when she was growing up. When you think about it, it's amazing Allegra has come through so wonderfully well. It's called *character*.'

Chloe couldn't have looked more forlorn. 'You're in love with her, aren't you?' she said, mournfully. ' I can see it in your eyes. It's no *arrangement*. No marriage of convenience. You're hiding behind that word. You *love* her.'

'Maybe I do,' he said, his silver eyes distant.

'Then she's going to make you suffer!' Chloe flared up, the brittle, attacking edge back in her voice. 'Just like Mark.'

'Why don't *you* marry him Chloe?' Rory suggested, wondering at her startled, maybe guilty expression? 'So long now. Have a good trip. I hope you learn something along the way. You might even consider striking out on your own when you come home.' He began to move off then half turned back. 'By the way, suffering with Allegra sounds infinitely better than setting up house with any other woman I know.'

The four weeks had been fairly peaceful for Allegra, though she found herself missing Rory with every fibre of her being. They kept in constant touch. For the most part he reported to her daily and she called him frequently at the Jimboorie pub where he was staying until Valerie and Chloe moved out. The last time he had spoken to her he told her he wanted her home.

Home!

She couldn't believe the momentum her life had taken on. Everyone knew of rebound relationships. They happened all the time. She was one hundred percent certain she wasn't on any rebound from Mark. What was happening was destiny. She was finding it incredibly exciting. She even felt truly young again as though she had been given a second chance to leave her unhappy past behind.

Mark had wounded her pride and self-esteem. With Rory she felt she wasn't so much taking a risk with their 'marriage of convenience'—she knew in her heart it wasn't—she was daring to dream. She wanted a husband she could love and respect; she wanted children before it was too late. If the timing appeared too soon after the breakdown of one marriage, to her it only offered proof there were miracles in life.

At some point on the way to her parked car, Allegra had the unnerving feeling someone was following her. She stopped, looked back a few times, but everything appeared normal for 5:20 on a midweek working day. Crowds jostled. Shoppers, laden with carry bags, made their way, heads down, for the underground city car parks or the trains. Office workers were spilling out of the tall buildings and onto the streets; eager young single women raced home to change for dinner or the theatre, their faces alight with anticipation. She would return to Naroom at the weekend. It was now Wednesday. Saturday couldn't come soon enough!

She had arrived home, relaxing in her apartment, sipping a glass of chilled sauvignon blanc and watching a current affairs programme when there was a knock at her door. Probably Liz Delaney, an art dealer, from the adjoining apartment. Allegra had promised to have lunch with Liz before she went back. They had become good friends over the time since she had moved into the apartment post her break-up with Mark. An outside visitor would have had to get through security so it had to be someone in her section of the building that contained six apartments.

She looked through the peephole. No one there. That was odd. A number of times she'd come home to find a parcel outside her door kindly delivered by the management team, husband and wife. Maybe they'd come by. She opened the door slightly and as she did so there was Mark! As usual he looked wonderfully well tended, expensively dressed, flushed and cheerful, holding a very beautiful bouquet of dark red roses and a glittering ribboned box.

'Ally! You're a sight for sore eyes!' He smiled at her broadly, pleasure surging into his voice. 'May I come in for a minute.'

'I'm sorry. That's out of the question, Mark. We're divorced, remember?' Allegra's expression wasn't in the least hospitable, although she quickly adjusted to the shock of seeing him. Mark's turning up like this wasn't so extraordinary. He had always thought his manners and his monstrous brand of charm could gain him entrée anywhere.

Could it have been Mark who'd been following her? Possibly but he had never been violent or dangerous.

'Oh, don't be like that!' he begged, still looking enormously pleased with himself. Another woman? 'I've got some good news I'd like to share with you. You're not going out, are you?'

'As a matter of fact I am.' She found it easy to tell a white lie.

'I promise to be out of here in under twenty minutes,' he said. 'I have a date myself this evening. A wonderful violinist is in town A young woman, very good-looking, which will make her appearance on stage all the more exciting. You know I'm thrilled to see you, Ally. You don't mind if I say that? After all, we were very fond of one another. You can spare me a few minutes, surely?'

Even as she queried her own judgement, she found herself letting him in. Why was that, ingrained politeness?

He handed the roses and the ribboned box to her,

still smiling as though he were riding the crest of a wave. Maybe he was remarrying? Anything was possible with Mark. She wondered if a phone call from her to his latest conquest might put a stop to it but reasoned with Mark's capacity for deception that wouldn't be a good idea.

'So what's the good news, Mark?' she asked, waving him into a chair while she set his offerings down on the kitchen counter. Her mobile was to hand if she needed it. He could take his little presents with him when he left. 'You'll have to be brief. I have yet to shower and dress.'

'You never answered any of my calls,' he said in a soft chiding voice. He had a very good speaking voice and he knew how to use it.

'No.' She didn't offer an explanation. None was needed. She had in fact given instructions to her secretary at work, not on any account to put him through. She had an unlisted number at the apartment, so that took care of that.

'You have to know I miss you terribly,' he said, looking at her with fervent eyes.

'That's not something I want to hear, Mark.' There was more than an edge of coldness in her manner.

'There's no one, absolutely no one like you,' he continued strongly.

'And here I was thinking you were about to tell me you're remarrying?' she scoffed, starting to feel very angry with herself. Her judgement about Mark had always been off.

'Listen, my girl!' Mark, a well built man, leaned forwards in the armchair, his attitude abruptly hardening. 'I don't think I'll ever get around to a second marriage, which is not to say I won't have women friends from time to time. I'd probably have stayed a happy bachelor, only you entered my life. So beautiful and so innocent, irresistible!'

Allegra's mouth went dry. 'Mark, this is all ancient history. And I'm *not* your girl.'

'Open your parcel,' he said as though that would surely soften her up. 'I bought it especially for you.'

She shook her head. 'Sorry. I'm not accepting gifts from you, Mark. My fiancé wouldn't like it.'

'Fiancé?' His expression changed dramatically. 'I don't believe you.'

She placed a hand over her eyes. 'Mark, it doesn't really matter if you believe me or not. I have a new life that doesn't include you.'

He looked shocked. 'I think you're just making this up. You want to punish me.' An odd look of weird excitement crept into his expression.

'From the stupid look on your face you're finding that incredibly erotic.' Allegra stared at him in disgust, ready to get rid of him. 'You haven't sought professional help, have you?'

'What a crosspatch you are!' he laughed heartily.

'*You're* the one who really needs it. Come on, 'fess up. You miss me. God knows I want *you* back.'

Allegra moved swiftly behind the counter and picked up her mobile phone, holding it up for him to see. 'Mark, I'd like you to leave. I can summon help in precisely half a minute and my fiancé will be arriving in under an hour. He won't expect to see you and I assure you, you won't want to be around when he arrives. I've told him all about you, you see.'

Mark came to his feet, looking deeply offended. 'Damn it, what is there to tell? I wasn't a wife beater. I wasn't a bully. I didn't abuse you in any way. In fact I spoilt you rotten. What's this fiancé's name?'

His smile now looked more like a snarl. 'He's not anyone you know, Mark. His domain is the Outback.'

'And you're going to live in that godforsaken wilderness with him?' His expression was utterly scornful. 'How long do you think that would last? A beautiful creature like you willing to ditch a glamorous career and a lavish lifestyle for life in limbo with a *cowboy*? I mean where's the bloody culture?'

'I'm not chucking it as you seem to think. And I'm not decamping to Mars. The Outback is in my blood. I'm addicted to the vast open spaces. You never could believe that, but it's true. Besides, the man I'm going to marry is an achiever, Mark. A potential empire builder. He's also a cultured, sensitive man. We have many interests in common. Quite apart from that I've done what I never thought I'd get to do. I've fallen deeply in *love*.'

Mark just stood there. When he spoke his voice was quite calm, even sober. 'Ally, my darling, it's just another one of your little self-deceptions. You don't seem to have learned a thing married to me. You're so young and ignorant of the ways of the world. If you're speaking the truth and you are thinking of re-marrying you'll only regret it. Despite everything you've done to me, I still love you. My God, didn't I prove it? You had everything you ever needed.'

'You should really have your head read, Mark,' she said wearily. 'You look so distinguished, so benign, but underneath I think you're mad. You can't love someone then betray them with extra-marital affairs. We had some happy times, but they were quickly over. Our marriage was a big mistake for us both. *I'm* over it.'

'Well I'm *not*!' he said and looked at her like a wounded lion. 'I should never have let you go. But even I got sick of your parading your virtuous ways. For all you know, this Outback hero of yours could beat you up. Who would hear you in all that isola-tion? Who would know? You're taking a far greater risk with him than you ever did with me.'

'I doubt it!' she said with certainty. 'He doesn't have a personality disorder. Now, Mark, please go, or you might be the one who gets beaten up. My fiancé is six-three, years younger than you and superbly fit. I don't want him to hurt you.'

But Mark stood glued to the spot. 'Give me a kiss for old time's sake,' he begged.

'Don't attempt to touch me,' Allegra warned. 'This is all so undignified, Mark.'

Real tears stood in his eyes. 'You won't come back to me? I promise I'll never deceive you again.'

Allegra turned the mobile phone to her and started to punch in some numbers.

'All right, all right!' Mark held up a hand. 'I'm going.' He began to walk to the door.

Allegra followed, hugely relieved, but at the last moment Mark whirled about, clasping her in his arms and rocking her back and forth. 'I'll always be there for you, Ally. Will you remember that?'

'We're divorced, Mark. End of story.' Somehow Allegra managed to get a hand around him and turn the door knob. 'If I never lay eyes on you again, I *won't* miss you. Now *please*, go, or you might be late for your concert.'

Even as she pushed the door closed after him, he was still protesting. Oh God! The last thing she wanted was trouble.

Allegra gave it a minute, then she stared through the peephole. Either he was standing back from the door or he had walked off to the lift. She'd already turned the dead lock now she stood with her back to the door for a few minutes trying to calm herself.

Surely he had gone? And damn! In her agitation she had forgotten to give back his gifts. The scent of the roses reminded her. Their heady fragrance was like a mist in the air. After five minutes her pulses began to slow. Mark wasn't a complete fool. His public persona of sophisticated businessman about town was important to him.

It came as a double shock to hear another rap on her door a few minutes later. She stood silent, waiting for another one. It came and it wasn't gentle. Lord, was she going to have to ring the police? She loathed scenes. She was a very private person. Had Mark really taken leave of his senses? Allegra tossed her long hair over her shoulders and walked purposefully to the door, half afraid of what she might find.

It wasn't Mark standing there. It was Rory.

My God, *Rory*!

She started to shake with excitement. She 'd almost forgotten how tall he was.

She threw open the door on a wave of euphoria, her face radiant. 'Rory, how wonderful! What are you doing here? Why didn't you let me know you were coming?'

If she was expecting a long, lingering kiss or even a hug, preferably both, she didn't get either. He didn't smile. He had reverted to the dark, brooding look. 'Hello, Allegra. I'm here.'

'Of course you're here!' She grabbed his arm and tried to pull him in, dismayed by the resistance she felt in his powerful body. 'What's the matter?' she asked in perplexity, her euphoria dropping to dismay.

'Aren't you going to ask me how I got into the building?' He let his eyes slash over her, taking in her long flowing hair and the informality of her dress—a lovely yellow silk caftan banded in gold.

She stared at him in consternation. 'Isn't it enough you're here in the room? Okay, how *did* you get into the building?'

'One hell of a shock, too!' He walked past her into the living room, feeling so incredibly rattled he scarcely knew what he was doing. This was a far cry from when he had started out, feeling on top of the world. Here was the woman who could so easily make his life or break it. He had known that from the beginning but his decision to put his trust in her had been taken at the deepest level. Now *this*! All his old insecurities rushed to the fore like an unstoppable torrent. 'I ran into your ex-husband,' he said, as if that explained everything. 'You know, faithless old Mark. Imagine that! What timing! He'd just come from visiting you as I was about to make my way up.'

Her face paled. Surely he couldn't think he had caught her out? That made her angry. Here he was pushing her away when she had expected to be hauled close. 'How did you know it was Mark?' she countered. 'For that matter how did he know it was you? Heavens, you've never laid eyes on one another.'

'Ah, yes, but intuition is an amazing thing!' He rounded on her with a high, mettled look. 'Chloe had given me a fairly good description of him as well.'

'Ah, yes, Chloe, my little sister and my best friend. I don't think.' She wasn't about to confide in him about Chloe. Not at this stage, maybe never. 'So what did you say to each other?' She was becoming more agitated by the minute.

'Do you think I'd tell you?' His tone was near cutting *Stop, man, stop! Stay quiet until you calm down.* But he couldn't. He was jealous and incredibly distressed. To be so high, then plunged so low was hell. 'It was man stuff. Or at least it was man stuff my side. I think poor Mark is still mopping himself up.'

'You *hit* him?' Allegra felt a real pang of worry. Mark was enormously vain about his appearance. He wouldn't be any match for Rory.

'Just a tap on the nose. Relax,' he said sarcastically. 'Are those his roses?' He whipped his dark head in the direction of the counter where the roses lay in all their glory.

'Yes. I f-forgot to give them back to him.' Despite herself, Allegra stammered. Surely he would interpret that as a sign of guilt?

'What's in the box?' He coolly scrutinised her when his blood was on fire. She looked so beautiful she filled him with a furious desire. He had missed her so badly. Then the ex-husband appears. What was he supposed to think? The ex was giving notice of his intention to pay frequent visits? They could still be friends? What the hell was it all about? She let him in, didn't she?

'How should I know,' she answered him sharply, feeling goaded. 'I haven't opened it.'

'Let's open it now, shall we?' He strode off to the counter, the man of action.

Allegra spoke uneasily. 'I'd rather return it intact.'

'No, I want to see what sort of present he brought you,' he insisted. 'I seem to remember you're telling me once he was ancient history?'

'So he is. You're jealous?' She decided to do a little goading of her own.

'You bet I am, lady,' he clipped off.

At least that was good to hear. She began to settle. Jealousy she could handle. It was the lack of trust she couldn't. 'Surely you don't think I invited him here?' She gave him a cool, challenging look.

'He said you did!' He didn't rip at the glittering wrapping, neither did he lose any time getting it off.

'And you believed him?' She stared at him, horrified, fascinated, scarcely believing he was here with her. It should have been a wonderful reunion—she had been planning for it—instead they were into a ding dong fight.

'I didn't say that.' He realised calming down was going to take a little time. He had invested so much of what was in him in her. He had allowed her to become his heart, damn it!

'Well, that's okay then.' Allegra said, only half mollified.

'But you did very foolishly open the door to him,' he pointed out with a deep, vertical frown between his brows.

The atmosphere was starting to get very heated. 'So? I made a mistake. Haven't *you* ever made a mistake?'

'Of course. But I'm not going to make one with you!' There was desire in his eyes. And suspicion. Both equally intense.

'What is that supposed to mean?' Her voice filled with disdain. 'When are you going to decide you can trust me?'

'I was sure I *did*, God, Allegra, I thought we were committed to one another, then your ex-husband shows up. Well, what do you know!' He withdrew an exquisite and what had to be on the body a very revealing nightgown from its tissue paper wrapping, draping it over his hand. 'And look, there's a note to go with it. Isn't that sweet!'

'Give me that.' She made a little run at him, clutching for the card.

He easily fended her off. 'You can have it in a minute. I'm *dying* to read it.'

'Rory, I *hate* this.' She gritted her teeth.

'You think I'm enjoying it?' He held her off with one arm. "Couldn't resist this one," he read out. 'It's so exactly you, my darling. All my love now and always, Marko.' Marko? You called him Marko?' He raised infuriatingly supercilious, black brows.

'I hate to admit my poor judgement, but I used to think I was in love with him,' she said tightly.

'I'm so glad you used the past tense. When *exactly* did the loving stop?' His voice was a velvet rasp.

'When it was replaced by disgust.' She gave a brittle, self-deprecating laugh. 'Put the damned thing away, Rory. You're upsetting me.'

'Do you have any idea how *I* feel?' he asked. 'I couldn't wait for the moment I would see you again. I'm just wondering why,' he added unforgivably, but hell he was desperate. He studied the lovely garment carefully.

'How dare you say that!' Allegra fired back.

'Okay, I'm sorry. But we're supposed to be getting married remember?' He stroked the silk-satin beneath his fingers as if to calm himself. 'You wear things like this?'

'I *said*, put it back.' She made a futile clutch for it.

Somehow they were pressed together, both trembling with anger, and a sexual excitement that was gaining strength by the minute.

His handsome face held a searing mockery. 'I confess I'm not surprised poor old Marko got a bit out of hand.'

She stared back at him, devastated by the taunting in his eyes. 'Stop that right now.'

'Sure. We don't need to talk about him. I have to say I wouldn't mind seeing you in this myself.' He pulled her ever closer, desperate for that closeness, knowing where it was going to take them.

'I've missed you.' She hadn't meant to say it, but something in his eyes drew it from her.

His eyes raced over her face. 'You're telling me I'm important to you?' His tone couldn't have been more intense.

'Of course you're important to me,' she said fierily. 'I thought *I* was important to you. Or have you decided you don't trust me after all?'

He heaved a breath, his arms tightening around her. 'He told me you left him because you tired of him. 'Sadly I wasn't enough for her!' he said. He admitted being unfaithful to you, but he said you drove him to it. 'Ally's everything a man could ever want!"

She broke his grip, shocked by the force of her outrage. 'Don't talk to me about Mark Hamilton. He's a man who places himself above the rules of common decency. He's my *past*. Can we get that straight? Or does something in you *want* to believe what he had to say. No, don't deny it. You've got problems, Rory Compton.'

'Hell yes!' He hauled her back into his arms, 'I'd been counting on you to wash them away. So I was angry and confused…incredibly jealous. Is that so unusual in a man in love? But I couldn't have believed him, could I? Or else why did I hit him?' The tension in his body wouldn't ease. His face remained taut, his arms like iron.

Allegra swallowed. *A man in love!* 'He actually needed a thrashing,' she said. 'He's such a liar. All he does is *act*. I refuse to talk about him anymore. He's not worth my breath. When he came to the door I thought he was going to tell me he'd found someone new. Honestly he can play any role. I intended to give him back his damned presents but it was more urgent to get him out the door.' Deep hurt rippled through her voice. 'You so fear betrayal, don't you?'

'Don't *you*?' he retorted, his eyes trained on her. 'After your experience—'

'Hush, that's enough!' She laid a finger against his lips. 'The all important thing is I trust *you*. But if you're going to make a habit of jumping to the wrong conclusions it could destroy everything we're trying to build. Tell me where are we now?' Her blue eyes were ablaze. *A man in love?*

'Here together,' he said more quietly. 'I'm just a fool of a man. You have to keep that in mind.' His voice broke under the pressure of his feelings. 'God, I don't want to argue any more, either. I've gone beyond arguing.'

'That's good, because I—'

He could take no more.

Her breath was cut off under the exquisite crush of his mouth.

Rory recognised he hadn't been in control of himself or the situation after what had seemed to him an eternity of denial. He had missed her so much. Now the only thing he could do was communicate his driving need of her through his fervent kisses. He had never imagined he could be so jealous. He was ashamed now. He knew from this day forth he could never claim he knew nothing about male jealousy getting out of hand.

For long moments they were locked together, like a warring couple, each frantically aroused and taking what they wanted from the other. Passion crackled like a bush fire, spurting out of control. Somehow he was free of his jacket. His shirt was open and she had thrust her hand into the opening, her slender fingers stroking over his chest and tugging at the curling coils of hair. She was muttering something to him but he was so far gone, the meaning of her words wasn't getting through to him. Only when she gave a little keening cry did he draw back.

'I've hurt you?' He was torn between the need for restraint and the pounding desire to go on doing what he was doing to her.

'You've no idea how you've hurt me.' Sexual excitement had her shaking. Suddenly she was pummelling his chest, training blazing eyes on him. 'I hate you for doing that to me, Rory.'

'No one will ever hate me better.' He felt exultant, almost not sorry for what had gone before because it was so incredibly exciting to make up.

'Either you trust me or you don't.' She issued the ultimatum.

'I do trust you. Kind of.' He drew back a little, staring down into her beautiful blue topaz eyes. There was wild colour under her skin. 'Is it possible you've grown *more* beautiful?'

'Don't soft soap me!' she warned, trying to break away again. This wasn't going to be any easy submission.

'Come here.' He wrestled her back into his arms, not extending even a tiny part of his strength. Both of them were at fever pitch instinctively aware it had only one outcome. 'Don't let's talk, Allegra. Not now anyway. Talk is important, but I desperately want to make love to you. My body can tell you what maybe my words can't. But first, you have to tell me quickly. Can I?'

She drew back in amazement. 'You're asking permission? How quaint after the way you've been arousing me.'

'You don't feel you were arousing me back?' he asked with a dry laugh. 'Oh God, Allegra, I'm not asking permission. I'm asking if it's okay? I told you I want children. But I want lots of *you* first.'

His meaning suddenly dawned on her. 'Oh!' she exclaimed, starting to melt.

'That's a beautiful gown.' His tone was so gentle, but incredibly seductive. 'A caftan isn't it?' His hands slid caressingly over the silk that covered her breasts.

'Yes.' She gave a stifled gasp, unbearably excited by his touch. 'And you're changing the subject.'

'What was the subject? Ah, yes. Can I take you to bed?' His eyes lingered on her mouth, so luscious and cushiony soft. 'Or are you going to find the strength to resist me?'

Such a question when he could see how much she was in thrall to him. 'How vain you are, how arrogant!'

'Not true!' His mood was elation. He resumed kissing her, making every part of her come throbbingly alive.

Allegra had to softly moan at the sheer wonder of it. His hands began to move down over the long line of her back. They cupped her taut buttocks, lifted them slightly as he pressed the sensitive delta of her body against him, showing her the strength of his arousal. He was all man, all muscle, all effortless mastery.

She felt her eyelids flutter. She had never been so conscious of her most intimate parts of her body and the changes that took place in them under sexual stimulation.

'I love you in yellow,' he murmured, working little nibbling kisses down the graceful line of her throat. ' It does marvellous things for your colouring.'

Her trembling was increasing so much so she could barely stand. In fact without his supporting arms she thought she would simply sag to the floor. 'I'll remember that.' She spoke jaggedly. 'You really should have told me you were coming.' She was getting weaker by the minute.

'I wanted to surprise you.' The kisses didn't halt, but became even more passionate. His strong arms took more of her weight.

'You succeeded.' What wonderful sensory powers he had! She felt as though a man had never touched her before. She had read about heroines of fiction swooning away under the weight of desire but she had never expected to experience the sensation herself.

'So it's all right to take you to bed?' Urgently he lifted his dark head waiting for her answer.

'To sleep?' She hooded her eyes, teasing, tempting and luring him on.

'You can. *Afterwards!*' His face was shadowed with strong emotion. 'That's if you *want* to.'

She was leaning the length of her body against him one minute, the next he held her high in his arms. 'Which way?'

'Down the hallway, last door on the right.' Her voice was as shaky as if she'd run the four-minute mile.

The night was endless magic. They didn't sleep. They made love—*loving* each other—right through the long, moonlit hours. By the time dawn broke over the city each knew every centimetre of the other's body and what pleasure exploration could bring.

Gradually light filled Allegra's bedroom, turning the broad expanses of glass on the sliding doors to molten gold.

Rory turned to her, pulled her in tight and kissed her. 'You're so beautiful,' he said. 'I want to spend the rest of my life with you. I want to wake every morning with you by my side. I want to go to bed with you every night of my life. Will you marry me, Allegra?'

'Haven't I said I would?' She pressed her own kiss onto his mouth.

'Not a marriage by arrangement,' he said firmly.

'Never! This is a true love match. Heart, body and soul. You're my future, the love of my life.'

'Thank the Lord for letting it happen!' He released a deep, heartfelt breath. 'We're part of each other.'

'We *are* each other,' she smiled tenderly. After last night they weren't two people, but one.

'That's exactly how I feel.' He leaned back to the bedside table. 'I meant to give you this last night, but we sort of got carried away.'

'It was wonderful!' She lifted her arms ecstatically above her head, stretching like a cat.

'And it's not over.' He gave her a beautiful smile over his shoulder.

She held it, treasuring it, treasuring him. 'What are you doing?' she asked.

'You'll see. I want to do this right.' He threw back the sheet and stood up, a bronze sculpture come to life.

'Rory, what *is* it?' Those silver sparkles in his eyes thrilled her.

He looked for some clothes; pulled them on. 'Stay there.' He held up his hand as she made to move out of bed. 'You couldn't look more beautiful if you tried.' He came around to her side, kneeling down on the carpet. 'My first proposal was utterly unworthy of you,' he said. 'I thought in my damned foolishness I had to put it like a business proposition. I didn't want to frighten you off. This proposal is more fitting. It carries with it all my

love. Give me your hand, Allegra, love of my life.
You're everything I've been looking for and never
thought I'd find.'

Sometimes it was all a woman could do not to
burst into tears. She couldn't take her eyes away
from what he held in his palm. The slender hand she
extended to him was visibly shaking.

'As blue as your eyes,' he said, his face transfig-
ured by love. He showed her the sapphire and
diamond ring he had commissioned for her.

Her voice went suddenly very small. 'This is the
most beautiful thing that has ever happened to me,'
she whispered, her eyes huge in her creamy face.
Her hair tumbled around it and over her naked shoulders. Her breasts glowed in the golden wash of light.

'Our love is the one true thing,' he said, intensity
in his gaze. He began to slide the beautiful ring
down her finger to where it belonged.

'Oh, Rory!' Her eyes, glittering with tears,
outshone the precious stone.

'Do you like it?' His voice was gentle, his upward
glance full of desire.

She leaned forward to kiss his marvellous mouth.
'I *love* it. I'll never take if off.' Looking at him her
voice turned husky. 'You on the other hand have to
take off those clothes and get back into bed.'

He did.

CHAPTER EIGHT

THE Channel Country was in flower.

It was a magnificent sight, Jay thought as he sat his beloved motor bike looking out over the phenomenal floral display he'd rejoiced in since early childhood. The miracle of the flowers! Why wasn't Rory here to enjoy it! His brother's absence had all but stripped him of any joy in life. But there were moments like now to lift the heart. The sad thing was very few people over the short one hundred and forty years of settlement of the vast Outback had been blessed by 'the vision splendid.' Ah well, such was the remoteness of their pocket of the world!

Good rains after long periods of drought always did bring forth the most spectacular displays he recalled. The longer the drought the more dormant seeds lay ready to germinate. Nature took with one hand and gave with another. The man on the land accepted that. This vast, remote, sixty thousand square mile area, a major flood plain system, had been endowed with marvellous rain and they were all rejoicing. Their three giant sprawling rivers, the Diamantina, the Georgina and the Cooper that in the Dry flowed sluggishly for many hundreds of miles, sometimes barely flowing at all, had all but met up. The Cooper alone ran fifty miles wide carrying the overflow from the monsoonal rains in the north, more than a thousand miles away.

It was the massive interlocking system of drainage channels that gave his riverine desert home its name. The twisting, multi-channelled water courses crisscrossed fiery-red sand plains, dune fields, alluvial clay plains and even found their way into areas of the hill country. This was about as good as it got. All the neighbouring stations were ecstatic. Stations that went by formidable names: Nocatunga, Nocundra, Monkira, Malagarga, Mooraberrie, Moondai, Currawilla, Coorabulka, Turrawin, Turrapirrie, Kinjarra, Keerongooloo... The list went on. Cattle stations on both sides of the mighty Simpson Desert had long been regarded as the premier cattle fattening stations in the land. Not only did zillions of wildflowers spring to life after flooding, like now, so, too, did the native grasses and clovers, the golden Spinifex, the pearl-grey saltbush, blue bush, cotton bush and the valuable succulent, the pink parakeelya to fatten the stock. Long after the rains had dried up, and the sweet fattening herbage had disappeared, dry herbage was still delivering rich feed, packed full of nutrients.

It was to take advantage of the peak conditions stock from two of Turrawin's outstations had been trucked in. Cattle that had roamed far into the Simpson in search of feed during the period of drought were being mustered and brought back within the boundaries of the run. It made for a lot of backbreaking toil. There never was an end to it. Never life without the spice of danger. Because of the flooding, Turrawin had been cut off from the mail run for a couple of weeks, so he had yet to receive longed for mail from Rory, last stop a place called Jimboorie. He seized upon it knowing Rory would always keep him informed of his whereabouts.

A new overseer had been hired by the name of Mike O'Connor. He came highly recommended. Better still, because it made for stability, Mike was a happily married man with a wife, Janine, who had made a very comfortable home for them in the old overseer's bungalow. They had a young son they were very proud of who was at boarding school in Brisbane. He would be coming home for vacations. From all accounts the boy was thrilled his father had landed the job on historic Turrawin. A seasoned stockman, Mike was proving invaluable support. In some respects he reminded Jay of Rory, calm in any situation, clear sighted, fair but authoritative with the men. As soon as the waters totally subsided and the scattered stock were brought in he was determined on going in search of his brother and after that, who knows? Jay thought himself capable of many things, but running a huge cattle enterprise wasn't one of them. Sooner or later, their father would come to his senses. He needed Rory far more than Rory needed him.

For the first time Jay was serious about wanting to start an entirely new life. Rory was the rightful heir to Turrawin by virtue of his special skills and leadership qualities. Rory was the son to take over. Jay was happy with that. An uneasy truce existed between him and his father these days. Jay knew his father hadn't taken his intention to make a new life for himself seriously. His father didn't give him credit for anything much yet he had pushed both his sons to the limit. Rory had thrived even in adversity. Jay thought he couldn't survive much more of the harsh treatment his father dished out. As soon as he could, he was moving out.

'So how's O'Connor coping?' Bernard Compton demanded to know the very instant Jay set foot on the homestead verandah. It was midafternoon and he had returned briefly to get another pair of boots. The ones he was wearing had all but packed it in.

'Why don't you come see for yourself?' Jay suggested, so weary he slumped into a wicker chair.

'I just might do that,' his father said.

'Better than sitting around the house,' Jay offered mildly, as though the outcome was self-evident. 'It's downright unhealthy, Dad. What's happened to you in this last year? You seem to have lost all interest in station work.'

'Why do I have to work when I've got you?' his father returned acidly. 'And this new bloke.'

'But you've always been so active,' Jay persisted, truly worried about his father. 'Are you ill, Dad? Is there something wrong with you? Something you're not saying?'

Bernard Compton took a deep breath. Held it in. 'There's nothing in my life I can change,' he said grimly.

'What do you *want* to change?' Jay stared across at his father, thinking no matter how much he tried he would never understand the man. 'Are you upset about Rory?'

'I suppose,' Bernard admitted grudgingly. Rory was vigour, vitality, hell, he was even *rage*! Too arrogant for his own good.

'It's not too late to say you're sorry, Dad. Get him home.' Jay's tone brightened with hope. He knew he just had to wait and his dad would weaken.

But his father laughed at him. A cruel laugh. 'No, thank you!' he said adamantly. 'Better he stays away. I'm sick of him challenging me. If only you had some of his guts!' he lamented. 'But you'll never make it as a cattleman, Jay. You're always going to need a good overseer.'

Jay sighed, well used to hearing his father's dismal opinion of him. 'Got it, Dad. You've told me a million times. But you weren't so crash hot at the job, were you? Sure Rory's strong. He walks tall and he walks fearlessly. But he's in the mould of Grandad, not you. I'd give anything to see Rory right now.' His voice gentled with love.

'Just listen to you!' Bernard Compton laughed so hard he began to wheeze. 'You sound like a damned girl.'

Sometimes Jay thought his inner wounds would run blood. 'You're not the father I wanted, either, Dad.' He rose to his feet, thinking he didn't give a damn about getting his boots now. 'Why don't you saddle up a horse and come down to the camp,' he suggested, forever tolerant. 'We're at the Five Mile. Your skin is blotched and your eyes bloodshot. You don't look well. You've got to put a stop to your drinking, Dad. You're coming at sixty. The life you're leading makes you a prime candidate for a heart attack or a stroke.'

Bernard Compton's heavy, handsome face turned a burning red. He glared up at his son. 'When I want advice from you I'll ask for it, *Doctor* Compton,' he sneered. 'Now bugger off and leave me in peace.'

* * *

Jay jumped the steps and strode off to his motor bike.

He hiked a leg over the high powered machine, turned the ignition, revved the engine, then tore off in a cloud of dust and fallen leaves. There were still more hours of driving cattle out of some very rough places. The chopper was in the air. He preferred riding the bike to mustering by chopper, which could be very dangerous, or mustering on horseback for that matter. He loved his motor bike—he maintained it extra well—but he didn't look as good on a bike as Rory. Hell, he could never hope to be as good as Rory at anything. The thought didn't make him feel bitter, rather sad.

You sound like a damned girl!

He wasn't ashamed of loving his brother. God no! He loved Rory far too much for bitterness. It was the way Rory loved him. Why couldn't Rory have been the firstborn? He'd asked that question for years on end. Futile question but he asked it all the same. Even then Rory would have needed to look like their father and not their beautiful mother.

Mum!

Flying along at speed, the motor roaring with power, Jay was filled with gut wrenching memories. Jay was a young man who had always felt with too much intensity. Most of the time he was able to block his worst memories out. For some reason when he was physically very stretched, like now, they flooded into his mind. He'd better get a check on them.

How the grasses had grown! In some places they were long enough to hide a man. Turrawin looked simply amazing after the rains. When they were kids he and Rory used to stay in the desert overnight, tucked up in their sleeping bags, telling one another stories, staring up at the trillions of glittering stars. In the dawn they awoke, floating on an ocean of white paper daisies with seeds that would endure forever. When they arrived back at the homestead their mother would be looking out for them, gathering them into her arms.

'Had fun, my darlings?'

Abruptly Jay changed direction, some overriding pressure bearing down on him and clouding his judgement. He followed not the course of the waterway that ran past the Five Mile camp, but headed out across the sea of Mitchell grasses relishing the scent of new-mown grass that rose from beneath the crush of the tyres. A great flight of budgerigar rode the thermal currents above him; a fluttering V shaped banner of green and gold. The wind was whistling in his ears and whipping his hair back. Only then did he realise he had left his helmet back on the verandah. Hell that was a mistake. But his father always managed to upset him. His feeling was his father was ailing in some way. No point in suggesting he see a doctor. Bernard Compton was a desperately stubborn man. He could be his undoing.

Once Jay heaved up then lunged as the front wheel hit something concealed in the grass. The impact almost unseated him. Not quite. Still he punched the gas, as if he were recharging his own batteries. It was only at the last minute he spotted through the screening a big ugly rock rearing up out of the grass dead set front of him.

It was too late to jump it. He hit the brakes knowing there was very little he could do now to avoid being badly injured or utterly extinguished. The motor bike crashed into the rock with bone-jarring impact, the front wheel bearing the brunt of it. Jay felt his body rise metres up into the air as if he had grown wings. Perhaps he had! His body hadn't fallen. It was soaring higher, into an infinite sky that was lightening and brightening, turning into the most shining…incandescent…white.

As Fate would have it, it was the new overseer, Mike O'Connor, who spotted the overturned machine from the chopper. No sign of Jay. This wasn't the only nightmare Mike had lived through in his life. He knew from experience Jay's body could be hidden by the long grasses. Whatever had persuaded the young man to cut a swathe through that particular area deeply shrouded in long concealing grasses?

Mike hadn't found Jay in the least reckless. No rebel like his brother, Rory, who all the men spoke of with rough affection and respect. Rory, Mike had gathered, was the daring one. Neither Compton boys had been able to choose their ruthless old man.

'God Almighty! God Almighty!' A great lump stuck in O'Connor's neck and a rare rush of tears sprang into his eyes. Every instinct screamed this was bad. With anguish in his heart, Mike looked for a place to set the chopper down.

While this tragedy was unfolding, Allegra lay spooned against Rory's body, safe within the realm of his arm.

After that never-to-be-forgotten night, they had slept in. It was Saturday. No reason to get up. For that matter they could stay in bed all day. The very thought heated her skin. She held up her most precious ring to admire it. It suited her hand beautifully. It was the perfect symbol of their love. Very gently she turned her body towards him so that when he woke she would be looking into his eyes. Only she couldn't resist touching his face very softly, tracing a fingertip over the outline of his beautiful mouth. He had made her so happy she felt the tears swim into her eyes. Love with Rory was the sweetest, most meaningful experience, the distilled essence of her dreams. She knew she had been blessed with the greatest gift of all.

To love and be loved in return.

She must have drifted off again because she awoke to his warm lips against hers and his voice murmuring silkily. 'Time to wake up, Sleeping Princess.' The faint stubble of his beard deliciously grazed her skin.

'Lord, what time *is* it?' she asked, seeing heaven in those crystal clear eyes.

'Late.' He smiled back. 'But who cares. We can spend all day in bed.'

'Great! We don't need to get dressed at all.'

'Though we just might go out for a celebration dinner.' He kissed her again. 'So here we are.' He turned over on his back, taking a deep, voluptuous breath, then letting it out slowly.

'And it's wonderful,' she said, revelling in the flowing harmony.

'I've been watching you while you've been sleeping.' He drew her glowing head onto his shoulder. 'Even asleep you looked completely happy.'

'That's because I am.' It was so wonderful to be close. 'I've never been this happy in my life.'

'And it's highly contagious.' He kissed the top of her head, sharply aware of its clean fragrance. 'We're getting married.' He said it with enormous satisfaction, 'and it's got to be soon. Agreed?'

'Fine with me.' She snuggled even closer, laying the palm of her hand over his heart.

'We'll make it a wedding to dream about,' he promised her, his hands caressing her warm, silky flesh. 'Jay will be my best man.'

'Perfect!' she sighed.

He turned his attention to kissing her, engulfing her in pleasure. 'You taste of rose petals. I just *love* rose petals. I don't suppose you want to make love again?' he asked, with a quirk to his mouth.

She tilted her head to look at him. 'It looks like you can read my mind.'

'The wonder of you!' he said. One hand was in her billowing mane of hair, the other slipped down over her naked breasts. His handsome face reflected the depth of his emotions. 'God, how I love you! You're everything I want.' He moved back into kissing her while Allegra gave herself up to the mounting heat.

The phone was ringing. For a moment neither of them were able to surface. Then Allegra turned her head, staring at it blankly. Let it go to message, she thought. Rory, too, rose up on one elbow. 'Are you going to answer it?' he asked, his eyes glinting with wry amusement.

'I guess.' She swung her legs to the carpet and he moved up behind her, locking his arms around her hips and resting his face against her satiny back, pressing kisses into her spine. 'Hello, Allegra speaking. I'm sorry, I can't hear you. Fine, it's okay now. Carrie!'

Her voice was infused with surprise. 'What is it? Is it the baby?'

Rory listened as surprise was replaced by warmth. Then abruptly her whole body language changed. She had been pliant to his touch, arching her back for him, now he felt tension. 'Yes, yes, he is,' she said. 'He's right here. Yes, Carrie, I'll put him on.'

She spoke in such a strange, hushed tone Rory moved back across the bed and sprang to his feet. 'What is it?' He swiftly pulled on some clothes, knowing in his bones this was serious. Allegra turned her head to him, her beautiful eyes that had been so filled with sensuality now glittering with tears.

'Clay Cunningham wants to speak to you,' she said, holding out the phone to him, 'It's not good news, Rory, I'm afraid.'

'My father, my brother?' Rory asked urgently, brushed by premonition. Something in her eyes gave him the answer. Denial laced with heartbreak poured into his voice. 'Not *Jay*?'

'I'm so sorry. So dreadfully sorry.' Allegra reached for her robe, unable to stop the tears pouring down her face.

Life would change for them now that his beloved brother was gone. She remembered, too, grief had a way of shattering dreams.

* * *

Mourners came from all over, wanting badly to pay their respects. It seemed incredible that young Jay Compton was being laid to rest. Rory was home. Folk were soothed by that. God knows what the reaction might have been had Bernard Compton not called his son home. Never a popular man—most people thought Bernard Compton was full of black holes—he had been virtually ostracised since the news got out Rory had been banished from Turrawin. Didn't everyone know Rory Compton was the brains and the brawn behind the whole outfit?

He'd brought his fiancée with him, a most beautiful young woman who stood close beside him while his brother's body was being interred. On Rory's other side stood another beautiful woman. No one had any difficulty recognising her. She looked scarcely different from the last time anyone had seen her. It was Laura Compton, the boys' mother.

People tried not to stare, but they were fascinated, wondering how this was possible she was back on Turrawin, standing at her estranged son's shoulder. Everyone had thought all family ties had been cut but death had a way of bringing the bereaved back together.

Afterwards at the homestead the huge crowd of mourners had an opportunity to meet Rory's fiancée and offer their condolences to him and to his mother who met everyone's eyes directly and even attempted a few smiles. This would not have been possible, everyone thought, only Bernard Compton was not able to attend his son's funeral. He was lying in a hospital bed far away hooked up to monitors that beeped and hummed.

Bernard Compton had suffered a serious heart attack not twenty minutes after Jay's body had been brought in, felled by a massive burden of guilt. He had been air lifted out by the Royal Flying Doctor. Now he was being monitored in case of a second attack. Bernard Compton's only wish was for release. He had nothing left to live for. Death would only free him from the pain and the guilt. No parent should have to lose a child. That was the worst blow of all in life. He had never thought to lose Jay. He could only thank God he had never got around to disinheriting Rory. He'd lied about that. But look what it took to get Rory home!

To see them together, mother and son, was quite extraordinary, Allegra thought. Rory was the male version of his beautiful mother. No wonder the close resemblance had affected his father so powerfully. One could scarcely look at Rory—look into those remarkable silver-glinting eyes—without thinking of Laura. It was Allegra who had brought mother and son together.

Rory had reacted strongly when first she'd

brought up his mother's name. She had tried to proceed with caution but he was so stricken he could scarcely handle his grief….

'How can these things happen?' he raged, prowling around the living room of her apartment like an agitated panther locked in a cage. 'Jay loved that bike. He was always tinkering with it. Now he's gone when Dad goes on living!' He threw up his arms embittered and stunned by the thought.

'Your father's end might be closer than you think, Rory.' Allegra was sitting very quietly, watching him prowl. It was amazing the energy he was giving off for all his grief. 'At least he wanted you home.'

'Really?' He sounded angry enough to choke. 'Well, there's no one else, is there?' he retorted, his handsome features locked into an impotent rage.

'What about your mother?' she asked, always courageous.

He walked to the back of the sofa where she was sitting, resting his hands on her shoulders. 'What about her?'

'Shouldn't she be told?' She didn't back down, seeing it as a duty to him and his mother.

'Sooner or later, my love. No rush!' he spoke with extreme sarcasm. 'She abandoned us years ago, remember?' He released her to resume his pacing. 'Maybe I'll wait the same time and tell her then.'

Allegra rose and went to where he was now standing by the window. Her lover. Her life. She wasn't at all confident, however, she could sway him no matter what argument she presented. She put her arms around him instead, kissing his cheek tenderly. 'Come and sit down with me,' she begged. 'I know the agony in your heart, but you have to be strong to face what's ahead. '

'Don't I know it!' He slicked his dark hair back from his face. 'I know your compassionate heart, Allegra, but I don't want to see my mother. I don't want to see my father, either. Does that make me a bad person?'

'No, only human.' Very gently she steered him to the sofa. 'Still, your mother haunts you?'

His eyes went glittery. 'Why wouldn't she? She *is* my mother She gave birth to me and Jay,' he said more quietly.

'Come on, sit down.'

'I don't know what I'd do if you weren't here with me.'

'Well, I am. All the way. You'll *have* to see your father, won't you?'

The knots in his stomach tightened. 'I guess I have to show up.'

'It takes a big man to make big moves,' she said.

'I'm sure your father is suffering because of this. Not just his heart attack, but overwhelming feelings of guilt…of taking the wrong path in life. He's lost Jay but he did reach out to *you*.'

'When it's all too late!' A dark shadow passed over Rory's face. 'I'm past caring. This tragedy mightn't have happened had I been home. Jay wasn't in the least reckless. He was as aware of the dangers as I am. He must have been deeply upset about something. My father has a vile tongue.'

'It was his moment, Rory,' Allegra said in a sad voice. 'Jay's time was up.'

'It seems like it.' He searched her face as though it held all the answers he needed to keep going 'I'm not religious, Allegra. How could I be after this? I can't imagine life without my brother.'

'I know.' She took his hands in hers. 'He was very special to you.'

'Well, he's gone now.' Grief filled his throat. 'And he won't be coming back. The worst part is being so unprepared. I never got a chance to say goodbye. It makes it all so much worse.'

Her smile was strained. 'You mightn't believe this now, but some time in the future you'll realise Jay is around. You'll have these little moments when he's more than just a memory. He'll be walking right beside you.'

He gave a harsh laugh. '*You're* my only moments

of grace, Allegra,' he told her sombrely. 'Don't worry. I'm okay. I'll cope. It's just there was so much I wanted to say to him. Now I never will.'

'Say it all the same,' she urged, truly believing it would help. 'There will be ways to honour Jay, you'll see. I know you realise your mother might hear of his death from someone else?'

'Do you think she would care?' His handsome face was etched with misery.

'Of course she would!' Allegra found herself coming to Laura's defence. 'You told me when you were growing up she was a loving mother?'

That was met with silence.

'You told me she tried to see you after the divorce?' Her words continued at a rush. 'The visits went badly. All I'm saying is, some part of her is *still* the mother you knew. She's still *Jay's* mother.'

A turbulent edginess came into his face.. 'And it looks like she's got the woman I love for a powerful ally.'

She steadied herself. 'Being a woman I have to feel for her, Rory. More importantly, I'm trying to help you decide what's best. Please don't lock me out.' Her beautiful eyes were overbright in her pale face.

'As if I could!' His anger visibly cooled. 'Don't let's go on with this,' he begged. 'I can't contact my mother, not even for you, though you're mighty persuasive.'

'But it's you I'm thinking of, Rory. You spoke about missed chances. You won't get this chance again. I don't want you to suffer agonies later. Forgive me, but could I make a suggestion? Would you allow *me* to contact her? You said you knew where she lived?'

Rory's face was a study in conflicting emotions. 'I once stood outside her house, you know. I never went in.'

'When was this?' Hope quickened.

'A couple of years back when I was in Brisbane.'

'You wanted to talk to her?' She wanted him to go on.

'God knows why when there was nothing to say. We worshipped her. She left us. That's it in a nutshell. Jay was always the more sensitive one. I was the wild one, all mixed up. Jay had an even harder time than I did. My father's heart is made of stone.'

Allegra shook her head. 'That may very well be, but yours isn't!'

'We're talking about a man whose blood runs in my veins,' he reminded her with an ironic smile.

'There's a mingling of blood in all of us. It's possible your father has his own brand of love for you. He did, finally, give instructions for you be located and brought home.'

'So he did,' Rory acknowledged with a great sigh.

There was such an odd mix of expressions on his

face. Grief, anger, indecision and something she clearly recognised as the hunger he felt for her, and the comfort her body could bring. And why not? The same swirl of emotions were in her as in him. It seemed odd to be sexually aroused at such a time, but Allegra saw it as a reaffirmation of life.'

'Do you want to go to bed, Rory?' she asked gently.

His answer was a long, deeply felt groan. He reached for her, enclosing her strongly in his arms. 'That's what I want more than anything in the world right now. I want to feel *alive*! You and me!'

She was at the airport with Rory to meet his mother when she arrived. It was an hour's flight from Brisbane to Sydney.

'Loving you has made me a better person already,' Rory told her with a wry smile. He had thrilled her by consenting to making that vital phone call.

She laughed in relief, knowing that if she started to cry, she mightn't be able to stop. 'You won't regret it, my darling. I promise you.'

The instant she laid eyes on Laura, Allegra lost any tiny lingering shred of doubt. She didn't know exactly how the family tragedy had happened, but she was absolutely certain Laura had suffered as much if not more than her sons.

She was there when mother and son fell into one another's arms. The long estrangement just

vanished! Rory lost every vestige of the old bitterness as if it had been completely erased from his
mind. It was as though somewhere up there Jay was
already working miracles. Then Laura had turned to
her and taken her hand, holding onto it as though it
were a lifeline.

'Thank you, Allegra,' she said, her remarkable
eyes filled with tears. 'Thank you from the bottom
of my heart.'

Hadn't she just known what the exact colour of
Rory's mother's eyes would be! In fact Laura was
just as Allegra had pictured her. Time had been very
kind to her. She looked surprisingly young. She had
kept her figure, so her elegant pink linen suit hung
perfectly on her body. Her thick sable hair curled
softly around her beautiful oval face. Her smile was
lovely. She looked a *gentle* woman. One it would be
all too easy for a harsh man to hurt. Allegra took to
her at once.

Rory, too, had found his answer. It's never too late
for reconciliation. It's never too late to start a dialogue.
It only takes a letter or a phone call. Rory's heart had
melted at the first sound of his mother's voice.

Days slipped by after the funeral. They were alone
on Turrawin. A charter flight had been arranged to
fly Laura home but those few days together, though
filled with pain, had healed many wounds. Laura

had suffered just as badly as her sons when access to them had been closed off. The long silence she had so rigorously maintained now broke out of bounds. She told them stories of life with Bernard Compton, things Rory had never known or even imagined.

'It came to a time when I truly believed if I didn't leave Turrawin my very life would be threatened.'

It was impossible not to hear the stark truth in Laura's voice and to see the huge effort she was making not to break down.

'But you never said a word!' Shock glittered out of Rory's eyes.

'All I can do is beg you to forgive me.' Laura took her son's hand, immensely grateful she had been given this opportunity—however much grief surrounded it—to come back into his life. Had she not heard from him about Jay's death, she truly thought she wouldn't have been able to find the strength to go on.

'It was so incredibly hard for us all,' she said, her eyes full of sorrow. 'Bernard got incredible satisfaction out of making me suffer.'

'And he's going to have to answer for it,' Rory said.

But Bernard Compton's life was already running out.

That night Rory and Allegra lay in bed together, their limbs entwined. They had made the most extraordinary lyrical love in the moonlight, so close in body, mind and spirit Allegra thought of them as conjoined. Life was like navigating the open, unpredictable sea. There were the halcyon days to be treasured, the days the sea was rough; the times it turned pitiless, seemingly not to be overcome. They had encountered all three, braced themselves and somehow managed not only to survive but come out stronger and closer than ever.

The man they found in the hospital bed was a broken shell of the man he had once been. Weight had fallen off Bernard Compton's heavy frame so he looked fragile beneath the white sheet that covered him. He was very deeply asleep when they arrived. Rory had been notified to come. 'There isn't much time!' a nurse told him, looking deeply sympathetic.

Rory pulled up a chair beside the bed and took his father's slack hand. Allegra stayed at a little distance near the window. The pain of losing her own father descended on her like a heavy cloak. She remembered how dreadful it had been; how much she missed him. She resolved there and then she couldn't let Chloe walk away from her, even though Chloe had betrayed her. Chloe was her own flesh and blood. In time she would find a way.

Rory sat with his father's hand in his for a long while. So long Allegra pulled her chair close up to the bed. She didn't really like looking at Bernard

Compton as he lay there oblivious to their presence. She could see vestiges of his former handsomeness, but nothing of kindness. This had been a brutal man. Yet his own father, Rory's grandfather, had been much loved with a reputation for truth and integrity. It hurt her to know Bernard Compton's ruthless past had caught up with him. It had taken Jay's death to bring him to his knees.

To Allegra's eyes, it looked as though he had no hope of recovery. He looked like a man who had lost all will to survive.

It was deeply upsetting how much suffering he had brought into other people's lives, yet Rory was treating him gently. Just sitting there holding his father's hand as though he were much loved.

The same nurse's rubber soled shoes made funny squelching noises as she hurried down the corridor. There was a little irrepressible burst of laughter from a child and an admonishing, 'Be quiet, now, Hannah,' from a woman's voice. From the particular sound in it, it had to be the child's mother.

'He's gone,' Rory's voice startled her out of her sad reverie.

'Oh, Rory!' She placed her hand first on his shoulder, then leaned forward to touch Bernard Compton's arm. He was unnervingly cold to the touch.

'He's gone, Allegra,' Rory said it again, as though she doubted it.

Two short words, she thought, though there could be few worse to be told.

He's gone!

This will change our world, Allegra thought, and closed her smarting eyes. Rory would be master of Turrawin. That was his destiny. And what of her childhood home, Naroom? What would happen there?

CHAPTER NINE

ALLEGRA stared out over an ocean of bright yellow flowers. This was a world of a totally different kind to Naroom. Turrawin was *vast*! So new to it, it awed her. There were great flocks of kangaroos not in the hundreds she was used to, but thousands. They vastly outnumbered the people. Indeed the kangaroo population, some forty million, doubled the population of the nation. She had never thought it could be so exciting watching them bounding across the limitless plains in such numbers, no obstacle so high they couldn't take it in a flying leap. It was truly amazing to know a joey was only about the size of a bumble bee at birth.

The great flightless birds the emus, however, travelled not in huge flocks but in small groups. They made their nests on those plains, jealously stalking their territory and fixing anyone who came near with a baleful eye, although it was the male who had to stay home and sit on the eggs for an incredible couple of months. Emus could easily outrun the kangaroos and even keep pace with their vehicle. It was something to experience.

Great numbers of brumbies, too, roamed Turrawin in complete freedom. Allegra, the horse lover, found them beautiful to watch. The camels too fascinated her. In the one hundred fifty years since they had been introduced to the Outback by the Afghans the flocks had thrived in the desert conditions, increasing to two or three hundred thousand. Seeing them standing on top of a fiery-red sand hill had become almost as synonymous with the Red Centre as the big red kangaroos. She had to admit the giant goannas, the perenties scared her, especially when standing up they were taller than Rory. Only Indonesia's Komodo Dragon was bigger.

'They've been known to leap at the horses,' Rory told her. 'But at least they're not crocs! There are plenty of dangerous critters around here. Taipans, tiger snakes, death adders, the king brown. Scorpions. You don't mess with them. Snakes, fortunately, like to keep out of our way. The tourists are greatly taken with our lizards and we have the most in the world. Australia's reptile emblem, the frilled lizard is a big favourite. When something disturbs them the frill, which usually lies along their back rises in a big circle—about the size of a dinner plate—around their neck.'

'It's all quite staggering!' Allegra mused. 'The *distances*! I thought I was used to distant horizons, but this is overwhelming. The land has a completely different feel to it too. It's primal yet thrilling.'

'It's dreamtime country,' Rory explained. 'Aboriginal country. The colours of the landscape are Namatjira colours, the wonderful dry ochres he used in his paintings.'

'Like the ones back at the homestead?'

'My mother bought those,' he said. 'I should give them to her.'

'You could,' Allegra agreed, 'but she'll be visiting often enough. I used to think those burnt umbers, the cinnabar, lapis lazuli, indigo, vermilion were too vivid to be true, but they're not. They're very closely observed.'

So, too, was the cloudless crystal-blue of the sky; the fiery-red of the sand hills at their door, the stark-white trunks of the ghost gums she thought so lovely. But what struck her most of all was the birdlife. Watching thousands upon thousands of them congregate at the bores, a favourite meeting place was an unforgettable sight. Orange and red chats, zebra finches, countless species of parrots, galahs, sulphur crested cockatoos, the marvellous little emerald and gold gems, the lovebirds, the aboriginal budgerigar. It was magic and Allegra abandoned herself to Turrawin's spell.

Rory had sent their overseer, the man who had found Jay's body, Mike O'Connor to take charge at Naroom. He had already settled in with his wife, living at the homestead as caretakers. Allegra had met both of them, husband and wife, and was happy with the arrangement. Naroom needed a good man in charge and they had decided O'Connor was it. It had been decided, too, Naroom would form a valuable link in the Compton chain. It was part of Allegra's heritage so Rory had promised her it would never be allowed to go out of the family. Who knows a future son might want to work it?

'You'd better enjoy all this while you can,' Rory advised, running his hands lovingly across her shoulders and down her arms.

'It's a wonderland,' Allegra breathed. 'Could anyone believe on the driest continent on earth—right here on the edge of the desert—the entire landscape is mantled in wildflowers? I'm in awe of this place, Rory. It's so…'

'Haunting?' he suggested, a smile in his voice. 'The Great Spirits still roam this land. 'Be sure of it,' he said in such a voice it quickened all her pulses 'We're right in the path of the Great Rainbow Snake. The aborigines believe the spirits are beneath the earth, on it and above it. They believe someone, something, is always watching.'

'Well, it does have that feel.' She was ready to accept it. 'I believe in the Spirit of the Bush.'

'So do I!' Her deeply felt responses to his desert home gave him such comfort and joy they even managed to ease some of the misery Jay's passing had left in its wake. He mourned his father, too, but in an entirely different way. The what-might-have-been, the *if onlys*. A man was supposed to honour his father. He had certainly honoured his grandfather, but honouring his father had come too darn hard. Why was it some people were born full of a black fury? Was any of it their fault? All Rory knew was his father's death had come as a release. Not only to him, but to his mother, with whom he was reconciled, and in a way to the far flung Outback community.

Fate had made Rory master of Turrawin. To Turrawin's neighbours that seemed only proper and fitting. In Rory Compton they now had a neighbour and a helpmate they liked, respected and trusted. It was good to see him back at the helm; the place where he belonged.

Allegra sensed those feelings strongly when mourners came again to bury Bernard Compton in Turrawin's family cemetery, not far from his mother and father and his lost son. Bonds as strong as steel linked the people of the Inland. It was in part because of the *remoteness* in which they lived and part the national spirit.

* * *

'Just remember, you're seeing all this at its most magical,' Rory said. 'We might be carrying the fattest cattle in the nation at the moment but there are always the long years we have to get through the misery of drought. Far worse than anything you could ever have seen or suffered on Naroom. You need to know that. When the Dry returns all these wonderful everlastings will wilt and disintegrate, but the miraculous thing is they scatter their seeds far and wide. The birds help out, so do the desert winds. They pick the seeds up and blow them even further.'

'Hence mile after mile of desert flowers,' she said dreamily, resting contentedly against him.

He dropped a kiss on her smooth cheek then let his mouth linger over her cheekbone. 'The seeds can survive years and years of drought and scorching heat. They're clever little beggars, too. They germinate only when a successful display is assured. A brief shower wouldn't trigger this miracle. Only good rains and flooding have achieved this.'

'So we live here.'

'You're not going to tell me you don't really want to?' For an instant his heart turned over in his chest.

'Just teasing!' She gave a little laugh. 'Whither thou goest, I go. You've promised me my beautiful Taroom will stay in the family. I'm content with that.'

He nodded. 'Incidentally I have all sorts of plans for it I want to share with you.'

'Good,' she said cheerfully. 'Sharing is what it's all about.'

They stayed there for some time revelling in the urgent ecstasy of the desert flowering. For all the glamour of the city Allegra loved the wonderful wide-open spaces better. This was where she belonged. The desert country, too, was so rich in colour, laid on as vividly as a painting, she found it incredibly dramatic. These were the holy places, sacred to the aborigines. She could feel the powerful magic. Identify with it.

Rory pointed something out to her way to the North-East. She framed her eyes with her hands looking towards the silver-blue light that danced all over the vast landscape. 'It looks like an oasis,' she said. 'I can see a lagoon and palm trees. There are even people moving about.'

'Mirage,' he said. 'Fascinating isn't it? A quick-silver illusion. Do you want to go back to the house?'

'No way! I haven't come down to earth yet.' She gave him a smile of wondrous delight. 'There's something I want you to do for me first.'

'Just tell me.' He made a trail through the white paper daisies as he walked back to her side. Something about her expression enthralled him.

'Make love to me amid the flowers,' she said

softly, pulling him in close. The scene was set. The sky was so blue it was nearly violet. The rich red earth was covered by a glorious floral carpet one could walk on to the horizon. It was unbelievably perfect, a lovers' fantasy. Her fingers curled into the open neck of his denim shirt as she stood on tiptoes to kiss him gently, deeply on the mouth. She was such a happy woman and he had made it so.

Rory's eyes took on the sheen of silver coins in the sunlight. 'I'd be more than happy to, ma'am!' The vibrant tone of his voice held an embrace. 'I've never made love on a carpet of fragrant flowers before.'

'The first time with me.' She kissed him again, feeling as free as the air. Then a thought suddenly struck her. 'What if someone sees us?'

He laughed aloud. He was feeling like a prince in his own kingdom, his princess beside him. 'The only ones who are going to see us, my beautiful Allegra, have wings, like those little guys!' He lifted his head to mark another flyover of the ubiquitous budgerigar, a lovely light glinting off their emerald and gold feathers. They were heading towards the Pink Lady lagoon, one of the all time lovely places on the station. The two of them had visited it that morning to take in the exquisite sight of the cargo of pink waterlilies it was carrying. To cap off the entrancing experience they were witness to the ritual mating dance of a pair of brolgas who had performed for them on the lagoon's sandy banks.

'Don't keep me waiting, my love,' Allegra called to him as she sank oh so languorously onto the thick springy mat of wildflowers, then lay back. She held up her arms, her eyes brilliant with invitation.

'God you look beautiful like that.' Rory's face bore an expression of urgent excitement. 'I love you so much!' He fell to his knees, straddling her slender body. Gently he stroked her face, his expression breaking up a little as though to love was pain. Then quite unexpectedly he lifted his head and shouted in such a voice it seemed to echo around the hill country away to their west. *'I love you, Allegra!'*

'And I *hear* you!' She clutched him around the waist, laughing with delight while she pulled him down to her. 'For all our lives?' she asked very quietly, but with deep significance.

'For all our lives,' he answered with a fierce passion, as though reciting a vow that could never be broken except under pain of death. 'You're *my* woman!'

He heard her sigh, long and deep full of rapture. 'That's fine, because you're *my* man!'

'Then that's settled!' He gave a soft, playful growl then hunched over her; the all powerful male.

Passion licked along his veins like a flame shoots towards a powder keg.

'Isn't this glorious!' she cried, arching her body towards him with a sense of utter belonging.

'There's nobody like you,' he answered in a deep, velvety voice. He desired her so much he was in actual pain.

Swiftly, not losing a second, Rory began to peel off his clothes, feeling the desert air waft across his bare skin, cooling, caressing, fanning desire. To have her here among the flowers seemed to him so marvellous it was like an electric shock to his loins.

She was starting to undo her cotton shirt, fumbling a little with the buttons in her haste. Now he turned his attention to her and he shifted her hand away so he could have the infinite pleasure of undressing her himself. He could feel the delicious trembling that ran right through her body. Rejoiced in it. This was love. This was life.

Rory was overcome by a strong sense of destiny. It all seemed so beautiful to him it was almost a wedding ceremony. He was deeply, *deeply* committed to this woman. Everything in him craved what only she could offer.

'With my body I thee worship!' He intoned the line strongly as he bent to her. Then having stripped her he began to kiss her all over her beautiful woman's body so wondrously constructed for his loving. Kissed her until she was shaking and crying out his name.

'Rory!' The very air seemed to fracture into gold dust.

Both of them were overwhelmed by that extra-ordinary mix of ecstasy and agony that was so much an element of passionate lovemaking. Yet nothing in the world could have seemed more romantic to them. They were cushioned in fragrance. Drowning in it. The scent of the crushed wildflowers was sinking into the very pores of their skin. To be young and alive and in love.

Allegra could feel moisture gathering in the cleft between her legs. She was ready for him. She had only to wait for him to enter her, to fill her, to touch off the wild tumult only he could arouse. One day they would have a baby…then, God willing, more children. They would be born on Turrawin.

A great wedge-tailed eagle circled them three times, as though astonished by what it saw. Such strange creatures humans! Then it flapped its great wings and flew off, soaring ever upwards as it made its way towards its eyrie in the ancient hills.

Neither Rory nor Allegra marked the eagle's flight or the thrilling stretch of its wings. But an eagle isn't the only creature that can soar. As the two lovers climaxed they, too, were borne up into the radiant blue sky…light…light…lighter than air.

Love when it's true has its own powerful magic. It's the closest a man and woman can get to Heaven.

EPILOGUE

Jimboorie Annual Picnic-Race Meeting.
Two years later.

THE weather could hardly have been better.

After continuous years of drought, the good seasons had come. The best spell in ten years, and the whole Outback had come to life. The river flats and the flood plains of the Inland were covered in a riot of green herbage, one species with a sapphire-blue flower that grew so tall in places—up to seven feet—horsemen and cattle could disappear in it. The organisers of the annual event, one of the biggest and best on the social calendar—especially since Mrs. Caroline Cunningham of Jimboorie Station, had taken over as President of the Ladies' Committee—had chosen the first week of spring to take full advantage of the mild day temperatures and the balmy nights. As happened every year, a gala ball was held on the Saturday night, following the running of the very popular Jimboorie Cup in the afternoon with horses and jockeys coming from the cattle and sheep stations spread over a vast area.

The three pubs were full up with visitors. Outlying stations had accommodated more than their fair share of guests. The bulk of the crowd was station people, owners and their employees, but dedicated race-goers and those that liked 'one whale of a time' had come from all over the country, including the major cities. Many urbanite Australians, though they lived in the lush narrow corridors of the country's seaboards, really felt the need to identify with the vast Outback of their immense country. Attending the big picnic race meetings was a way of doing it.

A dozen and more private planes stood on the town airstrip and the town's streets were clogged with dusty four-wheel drive's and tourist buses. Outback people loved to party so with opportunities for them to come together limited, they ensured they made the most of every occasion.

This year entries in the race had been expanded to professional as well as amateur jockeys. Not as unfair as it might seem at first glance. The Outback riders, all station people, were splendid horsemen with a greater understanding of local conditions and the terrain, which was essentially a Wild West track. The field numbered twenty, the largest lineup since the Cup, sponsored by the pioneering sheep baron, William Cunningham, had begun in the late 1880s.

It was fast approaching three o'clock the traditional time for the running of the Cup, the main race. Caroline, who was to present the Cup and a fat cheque to the winner, made her way to the fenced off course—white post and rail—in time to see horses and riders showing themselves off to the crowd. Each jockey wore a numbered square on his back. Caroline's husband, Clay, the winning jockey for the past two years was riding his favourite Lightning Boy. Each year the competition got stiffer, this year in the form of Rory Compton master of Turrawin Station in the legendary Channel Country on Cezar. 'Kidman Country' as many people called the South-West corner because it was there when he was camped beneath a coolibah tree Sir Sydney Kidman, the original Cattle King planned his mighty cattle empire that at its zenith spread over more than one hundred thirty thousand square kilometres of the Outback.

Today rivalry was incredibly keen. This was the first time the committee had received an entry from so far a field but she and Clay had pressed their friend Rory into entering. Over the past couple of years they had all become close. Clay actually took all the credit for introducing Rory to his beautiful Allegra. The rest was history. Caroline had been matron of honour at Allegra and Rory's wedding; Clay, best man. In turn the Comptons were godparents to their wonderful little son, Jeremy, who everyone at this stage called Jemmy.

Caroline caught sight of them now. Because she'd had her special duties to perform Allegra had offered to look after Jeremy for her. Allegra had quite a way with children. Caroline could see her son's blond curls shining like a cherub's in the sun. He really was the most beautiful little boy. Everyone adored him. There was no sign of the terrible twos about Jemmy. He was the sunniest natured child and he just loved Allegra's new baby. Caroline could see him standing protectively beside the pram, one hand tucked inside it, no doubt holding baby's little fingers. Caroline's heart melted with love. Children brought such incredible joy into one's life. She was so glad, too, she had Allegra for a friend. In fact she couldn't imagine life without her. Although separated by formidable distances, the fact Rory flew his own plane made it so much easier for two young married women to see one another fairly frequently when she and Clay visited. Both of them had been staying at Turrawin homestead the night Allegra gave birth to her daughter after a trouble-free pregnancy.

Could she ever forget the look of love and pride on the parents' faces! Caroline still had a lump in her throat at the memory.

* * *

Contentment written all over her, Allegra turned her head as Caroline hurried up to them. 'Hi, you're in good time!' Allegra's smile was radiant. Always beautiful, motherhood had endowed her expression with a tenderness that lent an extra bloom. 'I'm so glad we came, Carrie. The atmosphere is really exciting and so friendly! Don't the horses look marvellous? Groomed to perfection. Our riders, too, of course!' she laughed. 'Don't let's forget them. You look wonderful!' Allegra cast an expert eye over her friend's lovely outfit, thinking it absolutely right.

'I try.' Caroline smiled back and ran a loving hand over her son's platinum-blond curls. 'What a good boy you are, Jemmy,' she praised him. 'I see you're looking after baby.'

'She's boot-i-ful!' Jem pronounced softly. He took the baby's hand and kissed it. 'I jess love her.'

Both women laughed tenderly, their minds irresistibly jumping ahead to the time when their children would come of marriageable age. Wouldn't it be wonderful?

'Oh look, they're moving to the starting line,' Allegra exclaimed. 'Come on, my darling,' She swooped to lift her six-month-old daughter out of the pram and hold her up. 'Look at Daddy. There he is, sweetheart—Number 7. Uncle Clay is Number 4.'

Filled with excitement Jemmy began to jump up

and down. 'Wave, Jaylene!' he cried, trying to help her do it. 'Wave!'

The beautiful baby must have known what her little friend meant, because Jaylene threw her rosy head back and twitched a tiny hand.

Jeremy looked on in amazement and pride. 'Good girl, Jaylene!'

What other name could we have given our first child, Allegra thought, herself amazed at what appeared to be her baby's response. It was a name to honour the memory of the young man who was Rory's brother. It felt so right!

'Oh, it's so exciting!' Caroline said. 'I just love these days!' An excellent horsewoman she wanted to join in the race herself.

'Who did you back?' Allegra laughingly asked. 'As if I don't know!' Caroline and Clay were very much in love.

'The winner, who else?' Caroline's eyes sparkled with mischief. 'I just know this is going to be the most exciting race ever!'

And so it turned out.

A great full-throated roar went up from the crowd. Racing was the nation's passion.

'They're off at the start of the Cunningham Cup!' The race caller's voice came blaring over the loud speaker.

It wasn't the winning that mattered. It was the great enjoyment of Outback people coming together; feeling the kinship and the pleasure right down to the heart.

* * * * *

Turn the page for a sneak preview of
IF I'D NEVER KNOWN YOUR LOVE
by
Georgia Bockoven

From the brand-new series
Harlequin Everlasting Love
Every great love has a story to tell.™

One year, five months and four days missing

There's no way for you to know this, Evan, but I haven't written to you for a few months. Actually, it's been almost a year. I had a hard time picking up a pen once more after we paid the second ransom and then received a letter saying it wasn't enough. I was so sure you were coming home that I took the kids along to Bogotá so they could fly home with you and me, something I swore I'd never do. I've fallen in love with Colombia and the people who've opened their hearts to me. But fear is a constant companion when I'm there. I won't ever expose our children to that kind of danger again.

I'm at a loss over what to do anymore, Evan. I've begged and pleaded and thrown temper tantrums with every official I can corner both here and at home. They've been incredibly tolerant and understanding, but in the end as ineffectual as the rest of us.

I try to imagine what your life is like now, what you do every day, what you're wearing, what you eat. I want to believe that the people who have you are misguided yet kind, that they treat you well. It's how I survive day to day. To think of you being mistreated hurts too much. If I picture you locked away somewhere and suffering, a weight descends on me that makes it almost impossible to get out of bed in the morning.

Your captors surely know you by now. They have to recognize what a good man you are. I imagine you working with their children, telling them that you have children, too, showing them the pictures you carry in your wallet. Can't the men who have you understand how much your children miss you? How can it not matter to them?

How can they keep you away from us all this time? Over and over, we've done what they asked. Are they oblivious to the depth of their cruelty? What kind of people are they that they don't care?

I used to keep a calendar beside our bed next to the peach rose you picked for me before you left. Every night I marked another day, counting how many you'd been gone. I don't do that any longer. I don't want to be reminded of all the days we'll never get back.

When I can't sleep at night, I tell you about my day. I imagine you hearing me and smiling over the details that make up my life now. I never tell you how defeated I feel at moments or how hard I work to hide it from everyone for fear they will see it as a reason to stop believing you are coming home to us.

And I couldn't tell you about the lump I found in my breast and how difficult it was going through all the tests without you here to lean on. The lump was benign—the process reaching that diagnosis utterly terrifying. I couldn't stop thinking about what would happen to Shelly and Jason if something happened to me.

We need you to come home.

I'm worn down with missing you.

I'm going to read this tomorrow and will probably tear it up or burn it in the fireplace. I don't want you to get the idea I ever doubted what I was doing to free you or thought the work a burden. I would gladly spend the rest of my life at it, even if, in the end, we only had one day together.

You are my life, Evan.

I will love you forever.

* * * * *

Don't miss this deeply moving
Harlequin Everlasting Love story
about a woman's struggle to bring back
her kidnapped husband from Colombia and her
turmoil over whether to let go, finally,
and welcome another man into her life.

IF I'D NEVER KNOWN YOUR LOVE
by Georgia Bockoven
is available March 27, 2007.

And also look for
THE NIGHT WE MET by Tara Taylor Quinn,
a story about finding love
when you least expect it.

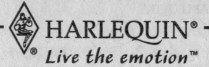

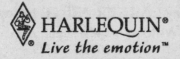

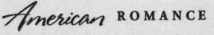
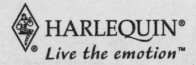

HARLEQUIN®
INTRIGUE®

BREATHTAKING ROMANTIC SUSPENSE

Shared dangers and passions lead to electrifying romance and heart-stopping suspense!

Every month, you'll meet six new heroes who are guaranteed to make your spine tingle and your pulse pound. With them you'll enter into the exciting world of Harlequin Intrigue— where your life is on the line and so is your heart!

THAT'S INTRIGUE—
ROMANTIC SUSPENSE
AT ITS BEST!

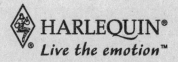

HARLEQUIN®
Live the emotion™